HANNAH'S HANKY

CLOVER CREEK CARAVAN

KIRSTEN OSBOURNE

ONE

March, 1852

Independence, Missouri

HANNAH MOSEBY SAT in the parlor of her step-father's home, quietly doing needlepoint. It was almost time for her step-father to be home, and she had no desire to see him. The man was absolutely insufferable.

Her father had died two years previously, and her mother had quickly remarried, though she hadn't needed to financially. They'd had a place to live and plenty of money to spend, but her mother had been lonely without a man in her life.

Hannah pitied her mother. She herself had no desire to marry anytime soon. Sure, all of her friends were marrying, because they were of that age. One of her friends was already a widow. Hannah had no desire to follow suit though. She was an independent young woman of nineteen years old, and marrying would only put someone in her life who thought they were allowed to do anything they wanted to her. Maybe someday she would marry, but that day would *not* be soon.

Her mother sat beside her, a shadow of the woman she'd once been. Mr. Gatlin had made sure she knew her place within their marriage from day one, and it was a place Hannah never wanted to be. A place of doing what she was told when she was told to do it. *No, thank you.*

Hannah looked up when the door opened, and she saw her mother jerk out of the corner of her eye, as if she was nervous now that Mr. Gatlin was home. Why on earth did she insist on marrying the crazy man if she was afraid of him? It made no sense to Hannah whatsoever.

Mr. Gatlin walked into the parlor where they sat, and he took a chair opposite the sofa. "Oh, good. You're both here. I want to tell you my good news while we're all together."

Mother looked up from her needlework and smiled at her husband, but to Hannah's mind it wasn't a real smile. Not like the smiles she gave Hannah when they were alone, or like the smiles she'd given to Hannah's father. No, this was a fake smile, reserved for her new husband. "What good news?"

"I have found a husband for Hannah. She is to marry a pastor tomorrow, and the two of them will leave for Oregon Territory on Monday." Mr. Gatlin looked proud of himself, as if he'd accomplished something Hannah was unable to do for herself. Of course, Hannah hadn't been looking for a man.

"I'm not ready to marry," Hannah said softly. "When I am, I will choose the man for myself." She looked back down at her needlework after the defiant words. She knew that Mr. Gatlin would be angry, and the man's face always turned a splotchy reddish purple when he was angry. She had no desire to see that.

"You're nineteen years old. Of course, you're ready to marry. You do not belong in this house now that you're grown."

Hannah frowned, waiting for Mother to say something —anything—that would make the man understand she didn't want or need a husband. But Mother sat quietly with her head down. This was the home she'd grown up in. It had been her father's home. If anyone didn't belong, it was *him*.

"I refuse to marry a stranger. Make other plans, Mr. Gatlin," Hannah finally said when it was obvious her mother would be of no help to her.

"I don't think you understand your situation, Hannah. You either marry this stranger, or you find someone else to marry in the next twenty-four hours. You are no longer a welcome guest in my home, and you will leave." Mr. Gatlin's face wasn't splotchy as it usually was when he was angered. It was downright evil-looking.

"But...this is my father's home! It was never yours." She couldn't stop the words from spilling out of her mouth, though she knew they would anger him.

"It is my home now, as I've told you repeatedly. The minister is coming for supper tonight, and you will either marry him or find somewhere else to go." Mr. Gatlin got to his feet, obviously very angered by her words. "I deserve thanks for finding a man who will happily take you off my hands, not your complaining. You are an ungrateful daughter, and I will be happy to see you go." With those words he left the room, storming off to his office and slamming the door behind him.

Hannah looked over at her mother, who was still staring

at her embroidery, obviously afraid to say a word. "Well, Mother? How are you going to convince him that I shouldn't have to marry the minister he found?" She knew her mother would have to be her ally. There was no one else to take her side.

Her mother shook her head. "I'm afraid I can't intercede on your behalf. By your age, I was married and had a three-year-old daughter. It's time for you to move out and become your own woman."

"Mother! You can't actually expect me to go to Oregon." Hannah was actually becoming frightened now that her mother had agreed with her step-father. How on earth would she be able to cook over a campfire? She knew how to cook over a proper stove, of course, because her mother had spent time teaching her. The servants usually did the cooking, but her mother had told her she needed to have the skill. She could also clean house and sew, but she didn't want to have to do those things. She liked being able to, but having to was something entirely different.

Her mother shrugged. "I don't really have a choice. My husband has said it must happen, and so it must." She got to her feet. "Let's go find a dress suitable for a wedding, and I'll talk to you about what to expect on your wedding night." Her mother blushed slightly as she said the last bit, and Hannah sighed. There was no getting out of this.

They looked through Hannah's dresses hanging in the chifforobe in her room, and her mother pulled out a beautiful dress she'd only worn to church one time. It was white and had beautiful sleeves that spread out over her hands. "This one, I think."

Hannah sighed. "Shouldn't I wear black to mourn the life that's being taken away from me?" As soon as the words were out of her mouth, she wanted to take them back. This wasn't her mother's decision. It was *that man's*.

"You need to be happy about marrying this man. He needs a good wife, and *you* will be that wife. You won't bring shame on me by acting like you don't want to marry him. Do you understand?"

Hannah nodded. "Yes, Mother." She didn't want to go. She didn't want to be a wife or a mother. And who wanted to travel the Oregon Trail? But there was no choice unless she could find a job as a domestic in town. That was a possibility. It was unthinkable though. She would be working as a domestic for her peers, and she knew she'd never be able to take orders the way a domestic should.

Her mother sat her down on the foot of her bed and sat beside her, pulling the handkerchief she'd always carried from her sleeve. "My mother gave me this the night before my wedding. She told me that marriage can be hard on women, but it's also a blessing. The handkerchief is to remind me that even if I cry some tears, I will always be blessed in my marriage." She held it out to Hannah. "I want you to have it."

Hannah hesitated for a moment before taking the object from her mother. "I will always treasure your hanky, Mother. Always."

Her mother smiled. "Good. Now, let's talk about what will occur on your wedding night. It's how babies are made."

Hannah was horrified as her mother told her exactly what would happen between her and her husband in her marriage bed. "I don't want to do that."

"Don't worry. If you don't like it, you can just close your eyes and plan your meals for the week. It'll be over before you know it."

"But I'm not ready for children!"

"You have no choice now that you're marrying. One of the most sacred things a woman can do is bear children. It was what God intended for us. I always wanted more than just you, but God didn't provide them for me." Her mother looked sad.

Hannah took a deep breath. "I'll do everything I can to be a good wife." Inside she knew she wasn't telling the whole truth. She'd never been good about obedience. Oh, she did as she was told the majority of the time, but she did so with complaint more often than not.

Her mother put her arm around Hannah and rested her head against hers. "I know you will." After a moment of sitting that way together, Mother got to her feet and said, "We need to get your things ready for your journey. You probably need to only take one or two dresses."

Hannah frowned. "I believe I should take them all. If we need something to trade along the trail, my dresses will work well." Truthfully, she just wanted to be well-dressed as she always had been. They could probably trade one or two of her dresses if there was a dire emergency.

Her mother nodded, looking at all the dresses her daughter had. She even had the dresses that she'd worn as a child hanging beside the ones she wore to parties and church. "We need to get started then. I'll go fetch a trunk from my room."

While her mother was gone, Hannah frowned. Would this be the last thing she and her mother did together? Packing up her clothing for an arduous journey that many didn't survive? She straightened herself up and began taking her dresses down. She would make it. She had to.

———

JEDEDIAH SCOTT KNOCKED on the door of the house he'd been told to go to for supper. He'd met a man earlier that day, as he was buying things for his trip on the Oregon Trail, who had told him he shouldn't go west alone, because there weren't a lot of women out west. He should instead marry the man's step-daughter. It seemed very odd to him, but he was more than willing. It wouldn't be easy to be a pastor out west with no wife.

He was nervous as he waited for someone to come to the door. He wasn't sure he would be interested in the woman, but he hoped he would. Of course, it seemed like providence that he'd been approached by a man in the local general store, so he would follow along. If God wanted him married to her, then he would marry her. He couldn't remember her name, but he was sure he'd been told what it was.

After what seemed an inordinate amount of time, the man he'd met earlier came to the door. "I don't know what happened to my wife and daughter. They usually come to the door. Excuse their tardiness, Pastor."

"It's no problem at all," Jedediah said with a smile. He had been invited to eat supper with this family and meet his future bride. He was looking forward to a good meal, but nervous about meeting the future wife. He hoped she wasn't too terribly homely, but even if she was, it was his job to do as God wanted him to do.

"Come sit in the parlor for a moment while I find my wife and daughter." Jedediah saw that the man looked very angry about something, but he couldn't imagine what it might be.

When Mr. Gatlin returned, it was with a woman who must be in her thirties. She was pretty in a quiet way. He was certain this must be the woman he was meant to marry. So be it.

"It's so nice to meet you," Jedediah said, nodding politely to the woman.

Mr. Gatlin gave him a strange look. "This is my wife," he said. "My step-daughter will be down in a moment. The two ladies were in a frenzy of packing, so I told Hannah she needed to tidy her appearance before meeting you."

"I see." Jedediah looked at the woman in front of him, whom he would have found perfectly acceptable as a wife. He had no idea what to say to her.

"I don't know your name, pastor," she said softly, and her husband gave her a glaring look.

"I'm Jedediah Scott. I just finished my schooling to become a minister."

"Are you traveling the Mormon Trail?" the woman asked calmly.

"No, I'll be traveling to Oregon. I don't know yet where God wants me, but I know it's not in the Salt Lake Valley. I'm not Mormon." The woman looked relieved by his words. "You weren't hoping I was a Mormon?"

"Not at all. I was hoping you weren't. I cannot imagine Hannah being married to a man she had to share with another wife."

Jedediah smiled. "Well, there's no worry of that at the moment."

"I'm glad to hear it!" She smiled slightly, looking at her husband with worry.

A young woman came down the stairs then, more of an age that he had expected for his bride. She walked slowly, but she seemed to be dragging herself, as if she didn't want this wedding that her step-father had assured him she would be in favor of.

She stopped in front of him and inclined her head slightly, waiting for something, though he had no idea what it could be.

He understood when her step-father made the introduction. "Mr. Scott, this is my step-daughter, Hannah."

Jedediah smiled. "I'm Jedediah," he said softly. "It's very nice to meet you, Hannah." He was pleased that she wasn't pretty. He knew that sounded strange, but with her red hair and freckles, she seemed to be only of average looks. He hadn't wanted a beauty for a wife, and he certainly wasn't getting one. She was pleasant enough to look at though.

"And you," she said softly, obviously knowing it was what she *must* say.

"Perhaps we could have a few moments to talk," Jedidiah said. "With the door open, of course."

Mr. and Mrs. Gatlin nodded, smiling at him. "I think that would be just fine," Mr. Gatlin said, following his meek little wife from the room.

Jedediah waited for Hannah to sit down on the sofa, across from where he was sitting. "I know this marriage is a surprise to you. I thought we could spend a few minutes getting to know one another better before the wedding tomorrow." He had to know she really wanted the marriage as he did.

Hannah nodded.

"I've recently become a pastor. I plan to go west and be minister to one of the underserved areas of the country. I enjoy being outdoors, and I'm looking forward to the long trek to Oregon."

Hannah blinked a couple of times. "You mean the long wagon-ride?" she asked. "We *are* taking a wagon?"

He nodded. "Yes, one of us will drive the wagon, while

the other walks beside it. I'm not sure you're strong enough to drive a team of oxen. Have you ever driven a wagon?"

She shook her head. "No, I haven't, but I'm certain that I could if I was allowed to."

He smiled. "I like your attitude. I'll teach you to drive on our first day of the trek."

"Really?" she asked. "You won't mind if I drive? You don't think it's men's work?"

"I don't think God cares which one of us drives the wagon, and which one of us walks beside it." He shrugged. "I don't know why He would."

"Then I would definitely like to learn to drive it."

"Sounds good to me. I wasn't looking forward to that aspect of the journey." Jedediah smiled. "Your step-father seemed eager to set us up with one another. Have you not met anyone else suitable?" The girl wasn't ugly, but she wasn't someone he would call pretty. She did have a nice shape and the dress she wore was pretty.

"I haven't *tried* to meet a suitable man. I thought I could stay here and grow old. My step-father told me that's not an option." Hannah looked straight at him as she spoke, and he felt sorry for her.

"You don't have to marry me if you don't want to."

"I've been told I marry you or someone else. I'm not allowed to live here any longer." There was no bitterness in her voice, but he sensed she was upset by the revelation she'd just received.

"Then marry me. I won't demand my marital rights until you're ready for them, and we will be a team working together to reach Oregon and all the wonders it has." He shrugged. "I want to be a pastor and a farmer, I think. My father was a farmer, and if I hadn't received God's call, I'd be helping him still. The farm would have been mine to inherit one day, but I have convinced him to leave every-thing to my younger brother."

"I...You'd wait on the marriage bed? My mother told me that men enjoy the act a great deal."

"I hope women enjoy it as well, but I know that's not always the case. I will wait until you feel comfortable with me and ready."

She smiled. "Thank you. I don't think you'll be a terrible husband after all."

He had no idea what she'd been told about him by her step-father, but he hoped he hadn't been painted *too* badly. He wanted her for his bride, but more importantly, he wanted her to want to *be* his bride. "I will do my best to not be terrible," he said softly. He stood up, offering her his arm. "May I escort you into supper?" He could tell she was a lady who was used to having men fawn over her. He wasn't going to be good at the whole fawning thing, but he was certain he could at least pretend to be a gentleman for a little while.

Her parents were waiting at the dining room table, and he pulled out a chair for her. He knew she was capable of doing it on her own, but it was a nice gesture, and one he thought she'd like. God knew once they started their jour-ney, it would be hard to observe the niceties of society.

Mr. Gatlin waited until they were seated before asking, "Did you get to know one another?"

"I believe that will take the rest of our lives," Jedediah said, "but we did some preliminary work on the matter."

Hannah smiled slightly. "I will marry this man with no complaints."

Her step father looked at her in surprise for a moment. "You will?"

"Yes, I will."

"Good then. I hope the two of you have a wonderful life together." Mr. Gatlin looked down the table at his wife. "What time would you like the wedding to be tomorrow?"

Mrs. Gatlin took a sip of the water in front of her. "I believe I would like a late afternoon wedding, if that suits the bride and groom?"

Jedediah nodded. "That sounds good. I will need to spend the morning getting my wagon loaded for the trip."

"And I'll need to spend the morning packing up my things." Hannah looked at her mother. "Do I have any dresses suitable for the trail?"

Her mother pursed her lips. "Maybe one or two. I'll make sure you have some before you leave, even if we have to buy them from the general store."

Jedediah frowned. It hadn't occurred to him that she might need clothes for the trail. "We're starting soon. Be sure you have plenty of winter clothes. I want to be nicely settled in Oregon before winter arrives, so we're leaving soon. Our wagon train will only be twenty-two wagons, and we're starting on Monday, the 29th of March. That's early in the year."

"That's fine," Mrs. Gatlin said. "I'll make certain she's ready. Let's plan to meet at four tomorrow afternoon at the church."

"All right. I'll be there."

Through the rest of the meal, Mr. Gatlin commandeered the conversation, and they talked about the perils of the trail. He kept emphasizing Indian attacks, but from Jedediah's information, the real killer was cholera. He didn't argue with the pompous man, though. He seemed to think he knew everything about the trail, simply because he lived in Independence.

After supper, he needed to leave right away. "I feel

funny leaving my wagon as long as I have. One of the other men on our wagon train, Joseph Mitchell, is watching over it, but he has two wagons and eight children to watch over. I can't take advantage of his time on the trail for too long."

Hannah got up to walk him to the door. "Thank you for coming this evening. Getting a chance to talk to you before the wedding was something I really needed."

"I can understand that. This whole thing is rushed." He smiled at her. "I'll see you tomorrow afternoon. After the wedding, we'll stop here and collect your things." Already he was thinking about the extra blanket and pillow he needed to buy for a lady. Hopefully she would have those things to bring, but her step-father seemed to be a singularly unpleasant man. He may not be willing to spare anything from his household.

"I hope you have a nice evening." With one last smile, she closed the door, and he smiled to himself. In a way he felt like he was rescuing her from a difficult situation. All would be well. God wouldn't have led him to her otherwise.

———

HANNAH SLOWLY CLOSED the door after him and leaned back against it, letting out a sigh of relief. It sounded to her as if Jedediah would be a good husband. The Oregon Trail wasn't something she wanted to travel, but hopefully it wouldn't be a horrific experience.

When she got upstairs to her room, her mother was already there, working on packing up her things. Hannah moved beside her and worked alongside her. "I bought myself a journal when I first married so I would be able to record everything about marriage and how wonderful it was. But you came along so quickly that I didn't ever write in it. I thought you might enjoy having it for your journey out west."

Mother placed a beautiful bound book in her hands. As she flipped through the pages, she saw that it was completely blank. "Thank you, Mother. I think this will be good."

Hannah had always enjoyed writing down private thoughts and little details about her daily life. She looked forward to writing down everything that happened on the trail. It would be such a wondrous journey that she was secretly excited about the time she'd spend on the road. Especially now that she knew she wouldn't have to walk.

Knowing that Jedediah was a good man made everything simpler. She didn't have to worry about him turning into Mr. Gatlin. At least she hoped she didn't.

She put the journal on her dresser, planning to begin writing in it the very next night. The entire story of her journey overland would be available for all posterity. It made her feel good to know that the things she did could shape the future for others. Why someday, they may even use steam engines to go from one end of the country to the other, but that was a long way down the road.

That night, as she put on her nightgown and braided her hair preparing for bed, she couldn't help but think about Jedediah, wondering where their lives would lead. Would she be the mother of a whole bevy of children? Or would she spend her life by his side as simply a partner and not a love?

She had no idea, but she liked that her life was now full of possibilities that it hadn't been full of even a day ago.

Maybe Mr. Gatlin was doing her a service, instead of forcing her into life of servitude as a wife. Only time would tell.

When Jedediah got back to camp, he walked over to talk to Captain George Bedwell, their wagon master. He had made the journey the previous year and found the area he wanted to settle in. He had come back for his wife and children, and all of them would be traveling together. His two boys, Harvey and Albert, were in their early teens, and they were very excited about the journey ahead of them.

"I just wanted to let you know that I'll be getting married tomorrow afternoon, so there will be one more on the trail with me."

Captain Bidwell nodded. "That sounds like a good plan. You'll be happy to have someone cooking your suppers in the evenings."

"I know that's true. She'll be here with me starting tomorrow night."

"Make sure she knows to bring warm clothes. Starting out this early in the year is going to make things just a tad bit more difficult on the beginning of the trail, but so much better at the end. I think we'll be glad we did it."

"I'm sure we will. I look forward to our travels." Jedediah walked back toward his wagon, saying a silent prayer as he walked, thanking God for Hannah and for her willingness to make the journey with him. He knew he was in for the adventure of his life.

TWO

When Hannah woke the following morning, she was both anxious and excited. Being out from under Mr. Gatlin's rule would help her a great deal, but it was more than that. She was actually looking forward to going adventuring with Jedediah. Once she'd met him, she knew he was a good man, and he was much younger than any preacher she had ever met. Why, she was certain they would get along like two long lost friends. She could already tell.

She spent the morning finishing the packing of her room with her mother at her side, and she found herself talking excitedly about Jedediah and the future she was sure they would hold. "Mother, he said we could be partners in life, and I didn't have to do...well, that thing you told me about right away."

Her mother gave her a surprised look. "He did?"

Hannah nodded as she carefully folded a blanket to take with her. She would take all of her bedding because her parents could always buy more. She had a feeling she and Jedediah would be having to be more careful with their funds. "He did. I really like him, Mother. Who would have thought that Mr. Gatlin would actually find me a man I wanted to spend time with? I think we'll start out as friends and after three or four years, maybe we'll actually fall in love. Then we can have children. I don't want to have a baby when I'm still a baby myself."

Her mother laughed and shook her head. "Despite the fact that you'll always be *my* baby, you're definitely old enough for marriage and children. I'll expect to get letters whenever you can send them."

It wasn't until then that it struck Hannah that she would be without her mother for the first time in her life. "I think you should come with me."

Mother frowned. "You know I can't do that. I'm married, and my husband is here. Besides, the pastor will not want his mother-in-law on the trail with him."

"I know you don't love Mr. Gatlin. No one could."

"That's not very respectful, Hannah. You're not going to be able to get away with saying things like that once you're married, you know."

Hannah made a face. "I think Jedediah and I understand each other."

"No man of God is going to understand you disrespecting your parents."

"I don't disrespect you. Just him." Hannah sighed, wishing she understood why on earth her mother had married Mr. Gatlin in the first place. He was over fifty and just plain mean-spirited. Unless he was in front of other Christians, and then he was a very pious man. It made her a bit sick to her stomach.

"Just be careful, Hannah. I've let you get away with disobedience to me over the years. Please don't be the same with your husband."

"I won't." Hannah wasn't sure what it would be like to

be married, but she was sure she'd have an equal say in all decisions. Jedediah would come to her. There was no reason for him not to.

An hour before they needed to leave for the church, Hannah's mother helped her change into the beautiful off-white dress they'd chosen for her to marry in. Her trunks were next to each other. Mother had helped convince her to only take two trunks instead of the four she wanted to take, but it had meant a lot of paring down to get to that number.

Hannah's red hair was fixed high atop her head, wound into a beautiful bun. "I wish I had blond hair. Or brunette even. I just hate being a redhead."

Her mother smiled. "Your hair is the exact same color your father's was. I saw his red hair in church one Sunday morning when I was about twelve. I pointed to him and said, 'I'm going to marry that man one day.' My mother just smiled, but I was married three years later. I so miss your father."

"I do too. It seems like forever since the day he hugged me goodbye and never came home." Hannah felt a tear drift down her cheek. "I wish he was here to give me away today."

"I do too. But Mr. Gatlin is planning to give you away, and you need to be kind to him."

Hannah sighed. "I will. But inside I'll be wishing it was Father."

"So, will I," her mother said as she pressed a kiss on Hannah's forehead. "We need to head downstairs now. He'll be waiting out front to drive us to the church."

Hannah looked at her room, now bare of her possessions. It didn't look or feel like the same place she'd lived her entire life. It was too...empty.

"I'll miss living in this little room and knowing you are

just down the hall. That if I cried out, you'd hear me and come running."

"I'll miss you so much, Hannah. You've been a daughter and a friend. I love you."

"I love you too." Together they walked down the stairs and outside to get in the wagon. Jedediah had told her they'd come by after the wedding to pick up her belongings.

Her step-father helped her into the buggy, and then he helped her mother. "I'm escorting the two most beautiful women in town today," he said loudly, so passersby would hear him and look at him. The man would do anything for attention. Hannah was surprised he hadn't had a banner made announcing she was *finally* marrying.

He drove through the crowded streets of Independence toward the church where Hannah's mother had married both of her husbands, and where Hannah herself had been baptized.

When Mr. Gatlin stopped in front of the church, Hannah waited for him to help her down from the buggy, knowing he would feel the need to do so in public. If there was no one around, he told her she didn't need help.

The three of them walked into the church, presenting a picture of a united family, though they were anything but in Hannah's mind. Jedediah was waiting at the front of the church, and she smiled as she loosely put her hand on Mr. Gatlin's arm, wishing she didn't have to touch him.

The pastor she'd had since she was a small girl was the one who married them, and when it came time for Jedediah to kiss her to seal the marriage, she lifted her face up to his, a bit startled. She'd forgotten about the kiss, and she'd never been kissed before.

She heard her mother weeping in the front row, and she

wished she knew how to calm her, when her own heart was trying to beat its way out of her chest.

Jedediah leaned down and briefly brushed his lips against hers, and she blushed, feeling strangely. His kiss had made her stomach tie itself in knots, but there was a short-lived fluttery feeling that she rather enjoyed.

She turned to face her mother and step-father and a few other people her step-father had talked into attending the wedding. She didn't know them, and she truly didn't much care that they were there. It was strange, but she had no desire to be around people that day.

She just wanted her mother and Jedediah. Hannah smiled at her new husband before heading toward her mother, who was still wiping away tears. She pulled the hanky her mother had given her from her sleeve. "This will help dry your tears, Mother."

When her mother saw the hanky, she cried even harder. Mr. Gatlin was looking at his wife as if she'd just grown two heads. "She's married. I thought you'd be happy now."

"I *am* happy," her mother wailed, crying even harder.

When her mother didn't take the hanky, she carefully tucked it back into her sleeve, wondering what to do about her mother, who was weeping and wailing as if she was Job and had just lost all of her family at once.

"Perhaps if we go somewhere more private, Mr. Gatlin." Hannah looked around and was very aware of the gaze of every person in the church.

Mr. Gatlin nodded curtly and got to his feet, leading her mother out by one arm. "Please stop making such a scene!"

Her mother only wailed louder at the words, and Hannah hid a giggle as she looked at the confused expression on Jedediah's face. "Mother *never* makes a scene. Ever.

This is the first time I've seen her cry in public. Even at my father's funeral, she remained completely stoic."

"Does she not approve of me as a husband for you?" Jedediah asked.

"She does, I think. But truthfully, she's spent very little time with you. She'll need a little while to adjust."

He frowned. "We leave on Monday. That's only three days from now."

"She'll be fine by then. At least I think she will. I will write often, and she won't even realize I'm gone." Hannah had always been particularly close to her mother, and she knew deep inside that her leaving would leave her mother bereft.

"I'm going to the campground to get my wagon so we can pick up your trunk. Do you want to walk over and ride back with me? It might be best if we leave your mother alone with Mr. Gatlin to calm her down."

Hannah nodded. "I'd like the walk." Mr. Gatlin had always tried to get her to stay inside and never venture out. He talked about how ugly freckles made her, and she was more prone to freckles than most because of her red hair.

"Let's go then," he said, walking toward the campground just outside of town with her.

She looked over her shoulder to watch Mr. Gatlin trying to help her still-crying mother into the family buggy. She wanted to laugh hysterically, but she wasn't sure how her new husband would react. She couldn't stop her lips from twitching though.

"You're amused?"

Hannah nodded. "Mr. Gatlin has no idea how to deal with my mother. He leaves every morning, and she tells me what's on her mind and we talk through it. He's not going to know what to do with her without me there acting as a buffer."

"Well, those letters will be fun to read, won't they?"

She nodded. "They certainly will."

As they walked toward the camp, he told her what he'd done already to prepare for the journey. "I'd already purchased all of the supplies recommended for one person on the trail, but your step-father gave me enough money to pay for a second person. So, I got everything for you. You have a trunk packed already, right?"

She nodded. "Actually, I have two trunks packed. I packed all of my dresses, because most have only been worn once or twice. I thought they might be good for trading on the trail."

He frowned. "I don't have room for two trunks in the wagon. Only one. You'll need to take fewer things to trade."

"But I had to work hard to only bring two chests. I wanted to bring four, but mother said two was more than enough."

"I agree with your mother. It's *more* than enough. You're going to have to get it down to one trunk and another crate. Nothing more."

"What? But I don't want to leave all of my special things!" Hannah quit walking and dropped his arm, determined to win this first argument with her new husband. He needed to know she wouldn't capitulate, simply because he was a man and he said so.

"Are you saying you won't leave more?" he asked, shocked that his sweet-tempered wife was digging in her heels so quickly.

"Yes, that's exactly what I'm saying. I don't want to leave my things, so I won't. It's that simple." She wasn't going to budge from her spot on the boardwalk without his agreement.

"You can't be defying me. We've been married only a few minutes and already you don't think you need to obey me?"

"If you wanted obedience, you should have married a dog. I'm far from obedient. I have a mind of my own."

He stood there, looking at her for a moment. "I'll let you keep most of your things, but our wagon simply can't carry as much weight as you're talking about. You could bring the things in the trunk, without bringing the trunk, and that would work beautifully."

She shook her head. "No, I want my things protected by the trunk."

"What if we put some of your things in an oil cloth bag? That would protect them from any damage, and you could still bring them, just not with the weight of a trunk?"

She considered it for a moment and finally nodded. "Yes, that should work nicely. Thank you for working out a compromise with me."

"I hope you know I won't always be able to compromise that way. You will need to be obedient for the most part."

"My mother is obedient to Mr. Gatlin, and she seems to have lost herself in that obedience. Where there used to be a woman who would laugh and joke and have fun, now there is this meek little thing that responds to everything her husband wants and needs."

He looked at her for a moment, thinking about what she'd said. He'd noticed her mother didn't speak much. "I don't want you to be that way. I just don't want you to try to argue with everything I say either."

"I'll do my best not to argue. I really will. But I think we should discuss things like rational adults instead of you just telling me how things are going to be. Why would I want to be tied to a man who thought he could think for me and run my life for me?"

He nodded. "I understand what you're saying. Shall we continue?" He offered her his arm, and they walked the rest of the way to the campground in silence. "I'll introduce you to Captain Bedwell this evening. I've already told him that you'll be joining our wagon train."

"Good. That will make things easier, won't it?" Hannah stopped in the middle of the circle of wagons. "If everyone is ready to go, why aren't we leaving until Monday?"

"There are many theories on the best time to start out for Oregon, and this particular wagon master thinks that April first is the best time, so we're waiting until Monday to go, which is still a few days before the first, but since he hopes to stop every Sunday for worship, clothes washing and to rest the animals, he wanted to start out a few days early rather than late."

"Does the month you leave in really matter that much? I've seen people leave as late as June."

"And some think June is better, but if we leave in June, there's no way we'll reach Oregon before snows fly. It makes sense to leave around the first of April to me."

She shrugged. "I guess that I don't have a real opinion on the matter. Would you be willing to go to my mother's house for supper on Sunday before we go? She'll want to see me one last time, if possible. We could always sleep there until we leave as well."

"No, I need to be with my wagon, and as my wife, you need to be with me." He walked toward Captain Bedwell's wagon to introduce her, hoping she wouldn't try and pick a fight with him again. She seemed to be a normal red head— one who would argue just for the sake of arguing.

The captain, his wife, and two sons were all sitting around their campfire. His wife looked a bit peaked, and they hadn't even started the journey yet. He could tell the woman wasn't going to do well on such an arduous journey. He promised himself he'd add her to his prayer journal that very evening.

"Captain Bedwell. I want to present to you my wife, Hannah Scott."

Hannah wanted to wrinkle her nose at the name, but she was able to control her reactions. It didn't seem fair to her that a woman gave up her identity to join with a man, yet he gave up nothing. "It's nice to meet you, Captain."

"And you, Mrs. Scott. The pastor here told me just last night he was getting married, and we're happy to have you along." He smiled a bit. "My wife is happy for every woman who joins the wagon train. She has been fretting for months that she would be the only one."

Hannah squatted down beside the older woman. "It's good to have other women along for me as well, Mrs. Bedwell. Are you feeling ill this evening?"

Mrs. Bedwell frowned. "I've never been in the best of health. I'm just feeling a bit poorly because of all the time we're spending outside."

"I can understand that. I guess it's part of life on the trail, though, isn't it?" Hannah promised herself she'd look out for this woman. She just didn't seem up to the journey.

Captain Bedwell laughed, a loud booming laugh that startled Hannah for just a moment. "She's a lot stronger than she looks. She's going to do just fine on the trail. You'll see."

"I hope you're right, Captain." Inside, Hannah was angry with the man for dragging a timid, sickly woman along with him. He certainly hadn't given her a choice, and that wasn't fair at all. Why did men think they had the right to run women's lives without them saying yes or no? It simply made her ready to scream.

Jedediah was already starting to be able to tell when Hannah was upset about something, and he knew she didn't approve of the captain dragging his wife along the trail with him.

He smiled sweetly at his wife. "Let's go get your trunk, my dear."

It seemed strange to Hannah to hear the endearment from him, but she wasn't about to argue. No, instead she'd go along meekly, since they were around people they would know. She would tell him exactly how she felt about the situation, but not until there was no one around to listen.

She wouldn't bring him shame with her forward-thinking ways, but she wasn't about to let people be mistreated without her husband getting an earful at the very least.

As they walked to their wagon, she was very quiet, trying to think of just the right words to tell him how she felt about things. When they got into the wagon and drove away from camp, her words were freed, and she no longer tried to swallow them.

"I don't think Captain Bedwell should be trying to take a sickly wife on the trail with him, do you? I feel deep down inside that it's the wrong thing for her, but he doesn't seem to care. Isn't he the man who agreed to love, honor, and cherish her as long as they both shall live?"

Jedediah took a deep breath. "I could tell exactly what you were thinking while we were at their campfire. Thank you for not saying anything in front of them. It wouldn't have gone well."

"I knew it wouldn't, and I wouldn't shame you that way.

I just think he's a horrible person for the way he treats her, and he should be flogged. There. Now I feel better for having spoken my mind. Don't you feel better knowing that I'm not hiding my feelings from you?"

He grinned. "You are a typical red head, aren't you?"

"And what exactly is that supposed to mean? That red heads have tempers? Well, yes, I do have a temper, and I'm not ashamed of it in any way." She crossed her arms over her chest and looked away from him. "Speaking of my temper, I think your name is too long, and I'd like to shorten it to Jed. Would you be amenable to that?"

He chuckled softly. "I grew up being called Jed, so the name would be just fine. It's much easier to spell as well."

She nodded. "I'm going to be keeping a journal of our travels. Mother gifted me a journal that she bought right after marrying my father, but she never got around to writing in it. I'd like to gift it to our children someday, and have it filled, so they could know how their parents' life was before they came around."

He nodded. "I'm keeping a journal of the trail as well. It won't hurt if we both keep one. It won't hurt one lick."

"I'm glad you agree. I'll start writing in mine tonight."

"I started mine when I left Illinois. I went to school there, and spent a month at home with my family, and then left for Independence. My professors told us that there was a huge need for pastors out west, so that's where I'm going. West."

"And as your semi-obedient wife, I'll go with you. Just don't expect me to pander to your every mood or act like I hang on your every word." Hannah shook her head. "When my mother started doing that with Mr. Gatlin, I was certain I'd vomit any moment."

He chuckled softly and stopped the wagon in front of

her parents' house. He knew now that he hadn't found himself an obedient wife, but he had found a spirited one. He wasn't sure which was better just yet, but he couldn't complain about the wife he had. She certainly seemed more suited for the trail than Mrs. Bedwell.

When they walked into her mother's home, she called out, "Mother, I need help!"

Her mother was there in an instant. "What do you need?"

"Jed says I'm not allowed to take two trunks. I can take one packed trunk and I can put the things from the other trunk in an oil cloth bag."

"I see. Well, I have an oil cloth bag that I use for transporting food to women who have recently given birth. I'm happy to give it to you. Let's pack up the bag." Mrs. Gatlin hurried off and came back with a large ugly bag, while Hannah dropped to her knees and opened one of her trunks. She quickly began removing things that would go into the bag, and put them in while her mother held the bag open. What had taken them hours to painstakingly pack now only took minutes as they shoved everything into the bag. "You'll stay for supper?" Mrs. Gatlin asked as they finished with the bag and she tied it closed at the top.

"No, but thank you, Mrs. Gatlin. Hannah would like to return for supper on Sunday evening, so she can say good-bye. Until then, we'll eat at the camp with the others in the wagon train. We're all getting to know one another, and it wouldn't be good if we weren't part of the time before the trail. We'll need each other once the wagons roll out, so we'll want friends." Jed explained quickly why they couldn't stay. It was as much so he could spend time alone with his new wife as anything else, though.

He hoisted the trunk onto his shoulder, and Hannah

put the bag over hers. "I'll see you on Sunday," Hannah said with a bright smile as she followed her husband out of the house. Life was getting strange very quickly. Soon, she'd be on the road with only the others in the wagon train for companionship. Hopefully there would be someone near her age she could quickly become friends with. She'd make it happen. Soon.

THREE

THAT EVENING, they had a small party at camp. One of the men Hannah hadn't met yet—James Prewitt—who went by Jamie got his guitar out, and played. Malcolm Bentley, a blacksmith going west to seek his fortune, immediately got his fiddle, and he played with Jamie. The two of them had obviously played together once or twice, because their music meshed nicely.

As soon as the music started, Jed held his hand out to Hannah. "Would you care to dance?"

They'd already stowed Hannah's things in the wagon, and Hannah had made her first supper over a campfire. She felt like it was an utter disaster, though Jed had eaten every bite and asked for more. He said he was used to his own cooking and very happy to eat something that wasn't burned for a change.

She smiled and nodded. She'd always loved to dance, though her step-father had decided it was wicked, and she hadn't been allowed to dance at all in the year that he'd been married to her mother. "I would enjoy that."

Hannah went into his arms, and he danced her around

the campfire to a wild, rambunctious tune. At the end of the dance, she had a stitch in her side and laughter on her lips. "That was fun, but I'm afraid I already need to sit down for a moment. I wasn't expecting such a wild dance."

He smiled, taking her over to the tree stump she'd been using as a chair. "They've played music every night for the past week as we've camped here. Sometimes people will pull out a deck of cards and play games. It's truly been a fun experience."

"I'm glad you told me we had to stay here then. I'm excited to know all the others we'll be traveling with. I hope we can make some life-long friends on this journey of ours. I'm not great at meeting people, though, so I might need your help."

Jed grinned, sitting on the ground next to her stump. "I think Mary Mitchell is about your age. She's accompanying her parents and younger siblings on the trail." He pointed in the direction of a young woman, who was sitting with a large group of children. "She's the eldest of seven or eight. I'm not sure which."

"Wow. I cannot imagine having so many siblings I was traveling with. Please tell me they brought more than one wagon."

He nodded. "There was a young man wanting to go west, Bob Hastings, and he's driving their second wagon. I'm not sure what the financial arrangement is between them, but a lot of families will hire someone to drive a second wagon, but they pay them in food."

She shook her head. "I can't believe I've lived in Independence my entire life, and I never knew any of the things you know about the trail."

"You had no reason to learn them. I wanted to know exactly what I was getting into." He shrugged. "Our wagon train is going to try to stop every Sunday, and I'm going to preach Sunday services."

"Oh! I didn't think we'd be able to have church on the trail. I'm thankful you're here." She smiled at him. "Well, since you're the only reason I'm going, I think I'm thankful you're here for that too." She felt a strange need to flirt with him, as she'd seen other girls do with men so often. There was just something about him that was awfully special.

He laughed, finding her much prettier when she was smiling that way. "Do you want to go around and have me introduce you to everyone?" He wanted her to be as comfortable in camp as he was.

She shook her head. "Not quite yet. We'll have time tomorrow, won't we?"

"Plenty of time. I'm thrilled with the time to get to know all the others, and even each other. Once we start on the trail, it's going to be long, hard days."

Hannah nodded. "Maybe you can spend some time tomorrow teaching me to drive the team as well. What did you name the oxen?"

"They're work animals. I didn't name them."

"What?" she asked. "We need to name them!"

He shook his head. "Next thing I know you're going to make me name all the other cows."

She looked at him with surprise. "We have *cows?*" Hannah had always preferred animals to people and knowing she and her husband had cows was thrilling to her.

"I'm taking three with us to Oregon. A bull and two heifers." He sincerely hoped she wasn't going to suggest naming the cows.

"We do need to name them then!" Hannah grinned. "I love animals. I had a cat before my mother remarried. Mr.

Gatlin said Mr. Whiskers made him sneeze, and I had to find him a new home. It broke my heart."

Jed shook his head. "I'm sorry you lost your cat." Hopefully, if he grabbed onto that part of the conversation, she wouldn't still talk about naming the work animals.

"So tomorrow, I'm going to need to meet all the animals. I want to name them all. Since you haven't done so, I'm going to claim the privilege for myself."

"Someone who named a cat 'Mr. Whiskers' doesn't need to be naming other critters," he mumbled.

"I heard that!" she said, glaring at him. "Mr. Whiskers was a perfectly good name. I refuse to believe otherwise."

He groaned. "Please don't make me drive a wagon pulled by Mr. Smart Hoofs, and his wife, Mrs. Smart Hoofs."

She giggled. "I kind of like those names. Do we have a boy ox and a girl ox?"

He simply shook his head. The woman knew nothing about farm life, and it was already obvious. "I'll introduce you to all of the animals tomorrow, and we'll make some decisions then." And he suddenly had an idea for the perfect gift for his new wife. He wouldn't say anything, because he might not have time to make it work, but he would try. "We have two days before we leave. We'll spend a little time tomorrow teaching you to drive the wagon, and we'll make sure you can find all the supplies easily. Are you a coffee drinker?" he asked.

She nodded. "Yes, I like to sip on it all day, warm or cold."

"Good. Rumor has it that people who drink coffee tend not to get as sick on the trail. I have no idea if it's true, but I'm certainly willing to drink only coffee if it'll make it more likely for us to reach our destination."

"I wonder why." Hannah had heard the same things said, but she had never been able to fathom what the difference was. What miracle was in the coffee bean to keep people living longer? Whatever it was, she would drink coffee and nothing else on their journey.

"Are you close to ready for bed?" he asked. He hadn't been paying much attention, but the camp was quiet now, and people were bedding down for the night.

"I need to write in my journal, and then yes, I'll be ready." She hurried to the wagon and climbed in the back, opening her trunk and removing her journal, an inkwell and pen.

Using her trunk as a chair, she opened the journal in her lap, dipped her pen in the ink, and began writing.

March 26, 1852

I married today. My groom is Jedediah Scott, a preacher. I've decided to call him Jed, because Jedediah is such a mouthful.

Our wedding was arranged by my step-father, Mr. Gatlin. At first, I was very upset at the prospect of marrying a stranger and being expected to travel the Oregon Trail with him, but now I'm excited for the adventure of it all.

Jed is a kind, caring man, who knows that I will never blindly obey him, and he seems content with that. I have no desire to turn into my mother, someone who has been completely cowed by her husband.

Tonight, we sat in camp, dancing to the music played by Jamie Prewitt (guitar) and Malcolm Bentley (fiddle.) Both are bachelors headed for new lives in the Oregon Territory. We leave Monday for this amazing journey, and we are thankful for the opportunity. I'm a little nervous, but I plan to be as careful as I can. I look forward to getting to know my new husband and all of the adventures we will encounter for the rest of our days.

After finishing her quick journal entry, she looked around her. Were they supposed to sleep in the wagon or on the ground outside? Suddenly, she missed her bed a great deal more than she'd imagined she would.

Digging in her trunk again, she pulled out a blanket, a quilt, and a pillow. She noticed that Jed had set up a small tent, and he was spreading his own bedding on the ground inside it, and that seemed logical for her. No one seemed to be worrying about wearing a nightgown, so she quickly changed into a simple calico day-dress her mother had made for her when she'd volunteered at the local orphanage in town, and she got down out of the wagon and laid out her bedding.

She put her bedding close to Jed's wanting to save him the shame of not sleeping close to his wife on their wedding night. She was not willing to participate in the marriage act with him—especially not with so many people around—but she wouldn't hurt his pride if she could at all help it.

As she lay on the grass, she shivered a little, and Jed raised his head. "Are you cold?"

She nodded. "I know we're close to the fire, but it's freezing."

He lifted one side of his blanket. "Keep your covers, but lay them over mine. Then we can share body heat. I think we'll be too cold otherwise." It was nice during the days, but at night, the weather got below freezing. He'd been dealing with it alone, but having someone to share body heat with sounded downright wonderful.

Hannah did as he asked, and moved toward him, covering him with the blankets she had brought as well as sliding under his with him. She had her arms clutched in front of her, trying to preserve her body heat as she shivered.

"Move your arms," he said, "down to your sides. If we lie with your back to me, we can share heat and be nice and warm."

She nodded, doing as she was told and rolling toward him. It felt strange to be held that way by a man she barely knew—or by anyone for that matter—but he was her husband, and she was cold. She wasn't going to worry about what they should be doing. No, she was going to be as warm as she could be.

Hannah's body warmed quickly, and she began to drift off to sleep, the feel of his arms around her making her feel protected. She could sleep that way for the rest of her life without complaint, and she just might do that.

Jed lay awake for a long while after her breathing had grown steady and she'd fallen asleep. He was surprised by how she'd acted that day. She seemed very different than she had the previous evening, but she seemed better. He didn't like that she hadn't obeyed his every command, but she was obviously very strong-willed, and he didn't see that as a bad thing.

He finally closed his eyes with a silent prayer to his Maker. "Thank you for sending this woman into my life. I already feel like everything I do is more meaningful with her beside me."

He buried his face in her hair and finally drifted off to sleep. His new wife was something special, and he would work hard to treat her as such.

———

HANNAH WOKE up to the sound of gunshots the following

morning and quickly became aware of the chill in the air around her. She must have fallen asleep with her window open again. As she stretched, she became very aware of a body behind hers—a very masculine body. Then it came to her. She was married, and she'd be sleeping outside for the next six months or so. It was going to be a very long journey.

She slipped out from under the cover and walked to the wagon, pulling a shawl over her shoulders for comfort. It was still cold in the mornings and at night, which would be part of the difficulty of this journey.

She took the stew she'd made for supper the previous night and carried it over to the campfire to heat it up. As she was looking for matches, she heard a voice from behind her, "What are you trying to find?"

Hannah turned and smiled at Jed, who was now propped up on one elbow under the blankets. "I'm looking for a match. I know I can't make a new meal every morning, but I thought it would be good to heat up what I made last night." She had thought hard about the best way to conserve her energy with cooking.

"We can do that today, but no one is going to wait for us on the trail as we heat up supper for breakfast. We'll have time to eat quickly and make a pot of coffee for us to drink on all day."

She sighed. "Cold stew?"

He grinned at her. "It could be worse. It could be cold beans."

She made a face. "I'll stop complaining."

He stood up and his body pressed against hers as he reached in and took the matches out, placing them in her hand. "There you go. I always put them back right there."

Hannah flushed as he pressed against her. He'd only kissed her the once, but she was starting to like feeling his body against hers. Probably more than she should. "Thank you. I'll start the fire and put the coffee on."

As she turned to head back to the fire, he stopped her, leaning down and pressing his lips against hers. "Good morning."

She blushed, and mentally berated herself for it. Everyone knew a red head was not pretty when she blushed. "Good morning." With her head down, she hurried to the fire, and set about her morning chores. She couldn't believe it, but she was actually anxious to be on their way. She could already tell how romantic the trail would be, with her and Jed sitting side by side in the evenings, holding hands and talking about their days.

As soon as they finished breakfast, he hitched up the wagon. "We're going to go have your first driving lesson," he said with a smile. "Are you ready?"

"I am. I like the idea of being able to drive the wagon and not have to walk along beside it."

He gave her a questioning look. "You know that driving will be hard work, right?"

"Well, it can't be nearly as hard as walking," she said.

"We'll see." He knew she was wrong, but he wasn't ready to tell her so just yet. It would be better if she came to that conclusion herself. There was no doubt in his mind that she'd soon be walking with the other women and the children.

Once the team was hitched up, he helped her onto the seat and drove a short way down the road that was the beginning of the trail. Finally, he stopped and handed her the leads, explaining how to drive. "If you let the leads go slack, the oxen will know they can go faster. If you make the leads tight, they'll slow down. You want to drive slowly down the hills and over rivers."

She swallowed hard. "Rivers? Can't we just build a bridge?"

Jed chuckled softly. "It takes months and sometimes years to build a bridge. No, we're going to have to drive across the shallower rivers, and even make canoes to go over some of them. I've heard that a lot of the pioneers will leave their canoes beside the trail, and whoever follows is free to use it. It hasn't been a particularly bad winter, so the rivers aren't very high. We should be able to just float across most of them."

"This is going to be a lot harder than I'm picturing, isn't it?" Hannah asked, shaking her head. "I'm not sure if I'm up for this journey."

He put his arm around her, pulling her toward him. "Of course, you are. You're going to learn a lot, and when you arrive, you'll be much stronger, both mentally and physically. It's not an easy trek, but it's worthwhile."

"I'll do my very best," she said softly.

"Now, give the leads a little slack and then start driving." He waited as she did as she was told, ready to take the leads from her at any time. "Pull to the right to make them turn."

It took every bit of Hannah's strength to be able to keep the oxen in line. By the time they stopped—after a one-hour lesson—she was aching. "I don't think I can drive the wagon. Does that mean I have to walk?" She hated the idea of walking, but her arms would never be the same if she tried to drive the wagon.

He shrugged. "I really don't mind if you ride in the wagon, but I think you'll find you prefer the camaraderie of walking with the other women. The wagon is very bouncy. From what I've been told, we can hang a bucket of milk on the bottom of the wagon, and we'll have butter by noontime.

I don't care which you choose, but I think you want to walk."

She frowned. "I've never walked further than my church. I'm not sure I'll be able to keep up."

Jed frowned. "Everyone is going to be sore on the trail. We'll be walking between fifteen and twenty miles most days. You'll find that you want to walk to be in good shape and to get used to the other women. You need to make friends."

Hannah was quiet for a moment as he drove back toward the campground. She'd had very few friends in her life. She was just odd enough that it was hard for her to make friends with other girls. "I'll try."

"You'll do more than try. I'm sure you'll find someone in camp that will become your lifelong friend. Go to one of the other women at lunch time, and ask them how to make biscuits over a fire. They'll be happy to teach you, and you'll get to know them during the process."

She sighed. "I'm really not ready for this trip, am I?"

Jed stopped the wagon in the same spot it had been in before. "I don't think anyone is really ready for this trip. It's long and difficult. People are being asked to do many things they've never done before, and that's not easy. I think it'll be a tad more difficult for you, because you weren't raised on a farm, doing hard chores every day, but you are just stubborn enough, that I'm sure you'll do great."

She frowned. "Did you really just call me stubborn? What kind of thing is that to say to a new wife?"

"Truthful in this case. I think it's one of my favorite things about you." He got down and came around, catching her around the waist and lifting her down. "Go find someone who looks nice and ask her how to make biscuits. We'll eat them a lot on the trail."

She nodded, wanting to complain. She'd been taught never to speak to anyone unless she'd been properly introduced, and he wanted her to walk around talking to strangers? Yes, circumstances were different, but it was still hard for her.

She walked slowly around the camp and spotted Mary Mitchell, whom Jed had pointed out the previous evening. She walked up to the other girl, noticing a musket leaning against one of the Mitchell's wagons.

"Miss Mitchell?" Hannah said hesitantly. "Could you teach me to make biscuits over the fire?"

The girl nodded. "Call me Mary, please. You're the preacher's wife, right?" She looked over Hannah's shoulder. "Ezra, I told you not to be climbing people's wagons. You're going to get hurt." Turning her focus back to Hannah, she said, "Sorry. Ma and Pa wandered off to the general store in town, wanting to stock up on a few things. That means I'm in charge of all of my younger siblings except little Maisie, who is still nursing, so Ma took her along."

"I am the preacher's wife," Hannah said, feeling odd just saying the words. She'd never dreamed she'd be a preacher's wife. "Do you want to go to Oregon? Or are you just going because your parents need help?"

Mary smiled. "Oh, trust me. I want to go. I want to have my own homestead. I'm not allowed to own land anywhere in the east, but I can there. No one can stop me, because women are allowed to own property there, even though they can't here."

Hannah smiled. "Well, aren't you clever? Do your parents know what your plan is?"

"Are you kidding?" Mary asked softly. "They'd tie me in a wagon to keep me from going to the deed office, but I just don't care. I want to be able to go where I please, not be tied to a man who will decide my future. That's not fair to anyone." She kept her voice low, and Hannah knew it was so people wouldn't hear what she was saying. A woman who thought like Mary did was not someone anyone wanted to be around.

Hannah lowered her voice. "I agree. I didn't want to marry at all, but my step-father decided I needed to marry Jed. If I have to be married to someone, he's a nice man, and I enjoy being around him."

"Well, that's good at least." Mary was mixing up the dough for the biscuits, and Hannah watched. It seemed to be the same recipe she already had memorized for the treat. "My pa has tried to marry me off a few times, but I always remind Ma how unruly the little ones are, and she tells him she can't do without me. Problem solved!"

Hannah laughed softly. "You're devious."

Mary grinned. "Just a little. Besides, no men back home really wanted to marry me, because I'm better with a musket than just about any man. I can't wait to shoot a buffalo!"

"Do you think we'll really see buffalo?"

"I'm sure we will. They're still roaming everywhere out west." Mary patted out the biscuits and put them into a cast iron skillet. "This isn't half what I'd make for my family, but it's about right for you and the pastor." Within minutes, she was pulling the skillet off the fire. "There, a perfect biscuit made over a campfire." She carefully removed one from the skillet and handed it to Hannah. "Try it!"

"I will. Thank you so much, Mary! And you *must* call me Hannah. I have a feeling we're going to be good friends."

"I think so, too."

FOUR

THAT FIRST DAY IN CAMP, Hannah talked to many people, but she kept going back to Mary. There was something about the girl that fascinated her and made her want to get to know her better.

Hannah shared the biscuit Mary had made with Jed when she got back to camp, and she made biscuits of her own that turned out just as good as Mary's. "Maybe I can cook over a campfire after all," Hannah told Jed.

"I never doubted you for a minute." They ate a meal of the biscuits with jam on them. Jed had purchased jam at the general store before realizing he would be marrying. He wasn't disappointed to have the sweet treat, though.

"What did you think of Miss Mitchell? I saw you over there with her and it seemed like you were enjoying yourself."

"I think I've found someone who will be a good friend in Mary. She thinks the same way I do in a lot of ways, but she was raised on a farm, so she knows how to do more things. She told me she can outshoot most men she knows."

Jed laughed. "I can see that the two of you would get

along well if she can do that. Does she even want to go to Oregon?"

Hannah considered telling him Mary's secret for a moment, but she couldn't betray her new friend that way. She had no way of knowing if Jed was friendly with Mary's father. "I don't think she really had a choice. Her parents needed help with the children, and she came along to help."

"Yeah, I think that's good of her, but I could see her not wanting to do it." He took another sip of coffee. "These are restful days as we make sure we're ready for the trail. Judging by the amount of jam you put on our biscuits, we may need to get a few more jars."

Hannah grinned. "I've never denied being fond of sweet things. I have a feeling jam may be the only sweet we get for a while."

"Then we'll need to walk into town and get some more. It's a long journey."

"I like the way you think."

He smiled, tracing her cheek with one finger. "I like the way you look when you have a genuine smile on your face. Your whole face lights up from within."

"That sounds positively ghastly. You don't need to tell me you like how I look. I know that I'm not a beautiful girl."

He wasn't sure how to respond to her without digging himself a hole for burial. "You're not a traditional beauty, no, but you have aspects that make you prettier than anyone I've ever seen."

Hannah shook her head and quickly washed the dishes from their small lunch. "I don't need you to lie to me."

"Of course, you don't. And I never would." Jed wasn't going to take back what he'd said, because it was true. There was something awfully special about her. "Would you like to walk to the general store for that jam after you finish with the lunch dishes?"

"I would like that a great deal." She wouldn't look at him though. Though his words were flattering, they made her doubt everything he'd said to her. She was anything but pretty.

On their walk, she pointed out different sites along the way. Places she'd been and things she'd done. "I've lived in Independence my entire life. My father ran the general store before his death. He was shot by someone wanting the money from the cash register. I wish he'd just given it to them. I miss him every single day."

"I'm sure you do. I don't know what I would have done if I'd lost my father. He's the best man I've ever known in my life, and I so want to be like him." Jed wasn't exaggerating either. His father had a passion for both God and farming, and he had a way of combining the two so you didn't know which he loved more.

"You understand then. Another man bought the general store from Mother, and he still runs it. It was hard to find a buyer at first, because of the shooting. Someone actually thought Father was haunting the store. I think that's just plain silly, but it still made it hard to sell." They walked into the store, and as she always did when she went in, Hannah looked all around, looking for the personal touches that had been there when her father was alive.

"I think we might want another tin cup for the trail. It was odd having to share one this morning," Jed suggested.

Again, Hannah worried about money. "I don't mind sharing." She didn't want to waste all their money before they even left for Oregon.

"We can afford another cup, Hannah." He walked to the shelf and pulled down a tin cup before walking over to the few jams they had on sale in one corner of the store. "Raspberry? Grape?" he asked.

"Both! Do they have honey?" Hannah looked around for a jar of honey.

"They do. I'll get all three, but these will have to last us until we get to Oregon."

An older woman stopped at their words. "Hannah Moseby? Are you going to Oregon?"

Hannah nodded. "Yes, I am, Mrs. Jenkins. This is my husband, Jed Scott. He's a pastor, and he wants to minister to those out west." She was glad she wasn't alone as she faced the old harridan who gossiped about everyone she'd ever met and many she hadn't.

"I hadn't heard you were getting married!" Mrs. Jenkins looked positively shocked that Hannah had found a husband. Hannah resisted the urge to kick the other woman as hard as she could in the shins, but she remembered how much it had embarrassed her mother the last time she'd done it.

Jed stepped forward and shook the offered hand. "It was fast. I took one look at Hannah, and I knew I couldn't go west without her." He smiled down at Hannah, a goofy grin on his face.

"Is that so?" Mrs. Jenkins looked skeptical. "I'll have to hear all about it from your mother. Why, I haven't called on her in ages. Not since..." Her voice trailed away as if she was afraid of upsetting Hannah, but Hannah knew the truth. She was trying to get a rise out of Hannah, and she refused to take the bait.

"Not since my father's death? When she needed her friends the most? Go see her. I'm sure she'll be happy to tell you everything you want to know." Hannah smiled sweetly. Mrs. Jenkins was a woman she frequently wanted to strangle. She walked around the older woman to the counter, where Mr. Hardy was working.

"Good to see you, Hannah. I heard you married some preacher man and headed out west. Your father was telling everyone." Mr. Hardy punched the keys on his cash register.

"That's mostly right. I married Jedediah Scott, who is a preacher, but we don't leave for Oregon until Monday. We're at the campground, ready to leave."

"Well, if that don't beat all. You married to a preacher man and taking off for the west. I know you'll be a great wife, Hannah."

"Thank you, Mr. Hardy." She'd always liked the man who had once worked for her father. He'd always paid special attention to her.

Jed paid for their purchases, and carried them out of the store in a small wooden crate. "Everyone knows you," he said. "And you didn't seem to like that woman who talked to you?"

"She's not a kind person. She's asking about me because she wants to be able to spread as much gossip as she can."

"I know the type," he said. "I'm sorry you had to run into her." He would have stayed between them if he'd known she would be a problem for Hannah.

"I am too. But I'm happy that I never have to run into her again!" Hannah did a little dance step as she walked beside him, and he chuckled loudly. "Are we going to church in town tomorrow?" she asked.

"No, I'm preaching at the campground. This will be my first week to preach for all of them. I got here on Saturday, and Sunday I preached for about half of the group, but now everyone is assembled, I'm actually a little nervous about it."

"Do you want to practice by speaking to me later? I sure

wouldn't mind." It wasn't something she'd ever expected—being a preacher's wife—but she was determined to be the best she could possibly be.

"Maybe. I'll practice it myself first, and then I'll decide. I'm not thrilled with what I've written so far." Jed had never found a sermon quite as difficult as this one.

"What are you speaking about?"

He sighed. "I thought I'd talk about how we need to be ready to minister to anyone along the way."

"Why not preach about God providing? Everyone is so nervous about the upcoming trip, a reminder that God will always provide whatever we need seems much more fitting. Matthew chapter six would be a great verse to center the sermon around."

A slow smile spread across his face. "That's brilliant. I needed an idea that I was passionate about, and this is one that fits perfectly with our situation. If my hands weren't full, I'd stop walking and kiss you right here and now!"

She laughed. "I wouldn't stop you."

"Is that so?" he asked.

"It is so. Maybe we can take a walk around the campground later, and you can demonstrate what you're thinking now." She knew she was being forward, but the man was her husband. If she couldn't be forward with him, who could she be forward with?

"I'm going to hold you to that," he said, grinning over at her. "Do you think we have enough jam now?"

"I sure hope so. Between that and the honey, we should be okay. I don't plan to do any preserving on the trip, so don't even ask me to." Thankfully, Hannah knew how. It was one of the things her mother had insisted on teaching her, despite the fact they'd had a maid and a cook to do those things for them.

"I wouldn't. We're all going to be exhausted on this journey. I won't ask you to do anything beyond the chores that you'll naturally get."

"Like cooking, fetching water for meals, and laundry?"

"Like all of those things. I know it seems like a lot, and it will be. I will do my best to keep up my end of the bargain too, and always keep your pots filled with fresh meat."

"Are you a hunter?" she asked.

He shrugged. "I'm not fabulous at it, but I do *enjoy* hunting a great deal. I won't try to outshoot Miss Mitchell if that's what you're worried about."

She laughed. "I hope not. I might ask her to teach me to hunt. I think I could be good at it if I tried." She'd found herself good at most everything she tried. That's why she was so drawn to Mary. As far as she could see they were very similar people.

"That wouldn't bother me at all, but you might want to have her do it today or tomorrow. There isn't going to be a lot of time for shooting lessons once we're on the Trail."

"I might just do that. I really like her. I hope you're right, and she and I become life-long friends. We could settle near each other, and our children could play together..."

"You know that most likely after we reach Oregon, we won't see the people in our wagon train again, right?"

"I know that, but let me keep my delusions. I don't want to have to think about making new friends again once we reach our ultimate destination. I want to imagine taking the friends I'm making now all through life with me."

Jed smiled. "I'm not one to keep you from imagining whatever you want to imagine." They had reached the campground, and they walked over to put the new goods in the back of the wagon. "I don't think anything else is going to fit, so I hope you have everything you want here."

"I'll make it fit if I need something else," she said with a smile. "I'm going to go over and talk Mary into teaching me to use a musket. I might bring in supper tonight."

Jed watched her go, noting the jauntiness of her step. She was so much happier now that he'd gotten her away from her step-father. He got out some paper, and he started to write out the new sermon she'd challenged him to write. It was going to be so much better than what he'd planned to say.

Hannah hurried off to convince Mary to teach her to shoot, and she found her new friend looking frustrated. "Are you all right?"

Mary nodded. "Yes, I'm fine. I'm about to take a walk to cool my head."

"Do you mind if I come with you? I was hoping you could teach me to shoot, but if it's a bad time..."

Mary grinned. "I'll make you a deal. I'll teach you to shoot if you'll teach me to fix my hair like you had yours yesterday. It was so beautiful."

"I would love to teach you! It's super easy, though my mother did it for me yesterday, because she wanted to fix my hair for my wedding. She said she'd been dreaming about how she'd fix it since I was a little girl."

"Sounds like a mother," Mary said with a grin. "All right, I'm going to let ma know what I'm doing, and that she's in charge of her own kids for a change."

A moment later Mary was back, and her musket was slung over one shoulder, with her two pouches of powder over her chest. She had a third pouch full of the balls that she would shoot. "The hardest part of using a musket—in my opinion—is simply loading it. Pointing and shooting are easy. I rarely miss, and only then if it's a moving target and I'm somewhat distracted. I cannot tell you how much I love being able to outshoot men around me."

Hannah laughed softly. "I know I'd enjoy it too, if I could do it. I want to bring in supper tonight. Is there any chance I could do that?"

"Sure. We're far enough away from town that we see deer regularly here. If not deer, we'll at least see a rabbit, and you could shoot that and take it back to camp."

"Sounds good to me." Though Hannah had never learned to shoot, she was very good at spotting animals, and she hoped it would help. They weren't even half a mile from camp when Hannah pointed off to their right. A buck was standing there sniffing the air as if he was trying to find danger.

Mary adeptly loaded the musket and pointed it at the deer, demonstrating for Hannah. Then she helped her friend hoist the gun—which was a great deal heavier than Hannah had expected—to her shoulder and showed her how to shoot.

Hannah carefully steadied the musket and closed one eye, trying to be sure she could see the buck. The recoil of the gun knocked her on her backside. She couldn't even tell if she'd hit the buck.

"You got him. He's lame now. I'll take the musket back and finish him. Good job!"

This time when Mary reloaded the musket, Hannah watched more carefully, determined she was going to be able to shoot. What if a bear came along while Jed was busy with something else? It would be up to her to protect herself.

Mary finished off the deer, and the two young ladies ran

toward it. "I can't believe I shot something on my first try," Hannah said, excited.

"I can't either. That was really good. Getting him in the hind quarter where you did was perfect, because it slowed him so I could shoot him."

"I was shooting for his head," Hannah said ruefully. She refused to not be elated though. She was bringing supper in with her friend.

When they reached the deer, Mary pulled a knife from her cleavage and proceeded to bind its legs with some rope she'd tucked into the ankle of her shoe. "What else do you have hidden on you?" Hannah asked. She had never seen a lady able to carry so much.

"Lots. I always have a knife in my boot. I keep ropes in various places. I'm not going to be caught unprepared. I sew pockets into all my clothes. I need to be able to get the things I need when I need them." Mary sighed heavily. "You must think me odd, being able to shoot the way I do. My parents had me and it wasn't until eight years later that my next oldest sibling was born. I'm twenty, and he's only twelve. So, my father taught me many of the things he would have taught a son, had one been born first. Now my parents both think I should become a shy retiring lady who only cooks and never hunts, but I've told them it's too late. I'm a hunter through and through."

Together the two girls dragged the deer back to camp. "I probably should have sent you back for someone with a horse," Mary said, "but it's just easier this way. I don't mind doing the work of pulling him back if you don't."

"I don't mind at all." Hannah's arms were already aching from driving that morning, but she wasn't about to complain. She felt as if she was doing something real by working side-by-side with her friend.

"We need to hang the deer in a tree for a bit to let it bleed out, but I'll show you how to get a good roast out of it. You can cook your man a fine meal tonight, and I'll give some to my mother to cook. I'm not fond of cooking, and she is, so we usually divide the chores with me taking on the little ones, and she does the cooking. We do the laundry together, though I'd love to find a way to get out of doing my share of that. It's going to be awful on the trail, when we have to tote water for it."

"Why will we tote water? Wouldn't it be easier just to do the wash at a river or spring? Whatever we find of course."

"That's a good point. My ma probably will think it's being lazy about our duties, but I think it's conserving energy for things we really need it for. Like walking beside those blasted wagons all day. I had to walk here from Northern Missouri, and I hated it. Especially having to keep the children calm and walking."

"I thought I was going to be able to drive the wagon, but I've realized there's no way on earth I can do that. My arms and shoulders are so sore from even *trying* this morning. Jed took me out and taught me to drive the team, but it was bad."

"I can understand that." Mary shrugged. "You can walk with me, and help me keep the hellions in line." She grinned at Hannah. "But my mother can never know I called them that."

Hannah laughed. "My lips are sealed. I didn't even tell Jed that you planned to get your own homestead when we got to Oregon City. I didn't want to betray your confidence."

"Thank you for that, though I wouldn't have minded if

you'd told Jed." As they stepped into camp, people spotted them.

Mary's father came walking over, shaking his head. "You always have to show everyone what you can do, don't you?"

"I was happy to get supper for the family tonight, Pa. My friend Hannah shot him first, and I just finished him off."

"Well, let me help you with it," Mr. Mitchell said. Hannah could see both pride and confusion on the man's face. As if he wanted to be proud, but it just didn't seem right that Mary could do what she did.

"I'm going to go tell Jed I shot our supper!" Hannah said with a grin. "Do I need to help hanging it from the tree?"

"Oh, no," Mary said. "Pa and I will handle it. We've done this together a hundred times over the years."

"You really shouldn't go bragging about your boyish ways, Mary." Mr. Mitchell shook his head.

Hannah hurried away before she could hear her friend's answer to her father. She didn't understand why the man wasn't prouder of Mary than he was. He didn't have to hunt or fish for supper, because Mary had already done it. Of course, her father had been proud of anything she could do. She almost felt badly for Mary, but then she remembered her friend was going to have a homestead all to herself.

When she got back to the wagon, she found Jed sitting on the tree stump she'd been using for a chair. "How's the sermon coming?" she asked.

"I'm almost finished, and I don't need to read it to you. I know it's what I need to say. Thank you so much for helping me with it."

Hannah shook her head. "I didn't do anything but

suggest a passage and a topic. You did all the real work. And I shot supper."

He grinned at her. "I saw you and Miss Mitchell dragging a deer into camp. You shot it?"

Hannah nodded. "I was aiming for the head, and I hit its hind quarters instead, but I slowed it down enough for Mary to finish it. We're sharing the meat with them."

"That sounds very fair. Did you enjoy shooting?" he asked.

"That musket knocked me on my backside," Hannah said with a laugh. "But I could do it myself now, and I think that's what's important. I want to be able to protect myself when you're not around."

He nodded. "I will feel much safer leaving you alone if you can."

She stretched her arms above her head, grinning. "I feel like I've learned a lot today. I can shoot a musket, and I can drive a team of oxen when absolutely necessary. And I can make biscuits over a campfire."

"You are so much more useful to me than you were yesterday," he said. The twinkle in his eye told her he was teasing, and she laughed along with him. "When you can preach a sermon, it will be time for me to just give up entirely."

"That's never going to happen," she said. "I wouldn't want it to happen even if it could." She had no desire to speak in front of people.

"I think you'd be better at it than you care to admit. You're afraid I'll put you to work doing my job for me."

"Not at all." She sighed, sitting down on the ground and spreading her skirts around her to carefully not allow any of her underclothes to be seen. "What will we do after supper tonight?" Already she was looking forward to spending time with him, and the trail seemed a little more exciting by the minute. Sure, she knew there was a great deal of hard work ahead of her, but she was going to do it, because she refused to fail.

"I thought we might seek out another married couple to play cards tonight. Would you like that?"

Hannah nodded, wishing her new friend were married. "Do only married couples play cards?"

"Oh, not at all. I know that Mary Mitchell and Bob Hastings will sometimes pair up for some of the games. I just watched those nights, because I didn't have a partner, but now that I have one, they would be fun to play with."

"Do you think there's some kind of romance going on between Bob and Mary?" she asked. She had thought so before talking to Mary so much, but now she was unsure.

"I don't. If there is something, it's all one-sided. Bob seems to be infatuated with her, but she has no interest in him at all. You can see it in her eyes. She's happy with what she does, and she doesn't really want to marry yet. When I first got to camp, I briefly considered courting her, but I could tell she wasn't interested at all."

Hannah felt a surprising pang of jealousy for her friend. "Would you have rather married Mary then?"

"Not at all. I married the woman I wanted to marry. I wouldn't have married you after meeting you if I hadn't wanted to. You are the right woman. I can feel it. God led me to you."

Hannah smiled. "I hope you're right." She couldn't imagine God wanting a preacher to marry her, but if He thought so, she wasn't going to argue with him.

"I know I am."

FIVE

JED'S SERMON went beautifully the following morning, and Hannah was pleased to see the reaction of the other emigrants around her. They all seemed to be happy with the sermon. A few of the men thanked him for preaching after the sermon, and Hannah was pleased that her husband's talents weren't being taken for granted.

As they walked back to their wagon for lunch after the service, she asked him something that had occurred to her during the sermon. "Are you being paid at all for preaching on our way to Oregon?"

"No, I'm not, but we'll be paid in kind. Different families will make us meals, and if a hunter gets something, and I don't, they'll share meat with us. It's more that we're all working together to make it there, and since I'm a preacher, I can share God's Word along the way. Perhaps it will help to keep people's spirits high."

"That makes sense. I'm still a little worried about Captain Bedwell's wife, but I guess she's going regardless."

"She is. You'll help her if she needs it along the way?"

he asked. He knew she had a heart for helping others, so the question was mostly rhetorical.

"I will. Of course. We're all a community working together."

"That's the attitude I was hoping you'd have." He sat on the stump while she made biscuits for their lunch. "What time are we expected at your mother's house for supper tonight?"

"They always eat promptly at seven. Not a minute before, and not a minute after." Hannah carefully watched the biscuits, making sure she didn't burn them.

"I take it that's your step-father's doing?"

"He's a very regimented man, wanting his meals and his clothes just so. I hope you're not that way when you're old like him."

Jed laughed. "I'll do my best not to be difficult."

"That's good, because I don't think I'd be as good about it as Mother is." She put three biscuits on a plate, and added a bit of butter to all three. Then she handed him the jar of jam they'd been eating from for lunch the previous day. "I think I may need to make biscuits every night for us to eat on the next day. Think we'll get sick of biscuits after six months?"

"I think if we still have biscuits in six months, we'll need to just be pleased that we have them, and that's that." Jed wasn't going to complain as long as he had food in his stomach.

"That's a good attitude. I'll work on being the same way," she said with a small grin. She'd never had to eat the same meals over and over, because their family cook had been quite creative. She needed to learn to accept what was available.

"Good. I wouldn't want to have to drag a complaining

wife all the way to Oregon." But he'd do it. Now that he was getting to know her, he wouldn't leave her behind for anything.

She chuckled softly. "I can't believe we leave tomorrow. It seems so fast."

"It won't seem fast when we're on the Trail. Your feet will ache, and most of the rest of you will too. You'll be doing a lot more work than you've ever done in your life."

"You're excited, aren't you?"

He grinned. "Just a little. I mean, I wish I could blink my eyes and just be there, but the journey is what has to happen first, so I will get there by any means necessary. And now that I'm married, I get a bigger plot of land."

"That's the only reason you married me, isn't it? You wanted more land. And here I thought you fell in love with my carrot locks the moment you saw me."

"Your hair looks nothing like carrots. You're more of an autumn sunset while the world is silent around you."

"Did you ever think about being a poet and not a preacher?" Hannah asked, shaking her head. "You have a silver tongue."

He shrugged. "I say what I think. Not a poetic bone in my body. If I tried to rhyme something, people would point and laugh at me."

"I wouldn't." She settled on the ground with her plate of biscuits in her lap. "Does anything else need to be done to prepare for the journey?"

He shook his head. "Nothing. We're going to try to make Sundays a day of rest, even on the Trail. Of course, that means you'll be doing laundry on Sundays, and I'm sure some of the men will hunt. It's not possible to have a true day of rest."

"I can't even fathom what it's going to be like, so why on earth am I excited? Am I just a bit deranged?"

"Everyone in this camp is. Or at least half of us. All the men. We're all going west seeking something, and all of the women are going along because they have to."

She sighed. "I hope it's not as bad as you make it out to be. I want this to be a good journey."

"It will be," he said softly. "I've been praying and praying about it. God will get us through. And that sermon today was a reminder I needed as much as everyone else did. You made a wonderful suggestion."

"I'm glad."

"Hello, Hannah. Preacher." Mary sank down onto the grass beside Hannah, and that's when Hannah realized she wore a split skirt. She wasn't having to be ladylike, because she was cheating. Hannah envied her for being able to do things that most women wouldn't dare try.

"Does your mother know you're wearing a split skirt?" Hannah asked, in a low whisper.

"Of course not. I made this skirt myself, and I always make sure I wash it. It's my favorite." Mary's eyes twinkled as she responded to her friend.

"We should make me one." Hannah had heard of the high winds on the prairies, and she had no desire to have her skirts fly over her head. Of course, she had a feeling Jed would think that was going too far.

"I don't know how you would be able to explain that to your husband. He's not going to look too kindly on a lady wearing a split skirt. And I have practice in hiding the fact that mine is split. You're the first person to notice in three years."

Hannah shook her head. "People aren't very observant then."

Jed looked over at his wife and her friend, a smile tilting the corners of his mouth. "What are you two whispering about?" he asked.

Hannah decided to answer him honestly. "I'm thinking about making myself a split skirt. It would look like a normal skirt, but it wouldn't fly up with the high winds."

Jed seemed to consider her words for a moment. "I don't think that's a bad idea."

Hannah looked at Mary with a grin. "See? He's the best of husbands!"

"I don't know how you'll find time to make one on the Trail, though," Jed added. "You're going to be too busy to worry about making skirts, split or otherwise."

She was determined to make it happen. "I'll do it during our lunches, and I'll do it while I'm waiting for supper to cook. And while I'm waiting for clothes to dry."

He laughed. "It seems you've thought about this a great deal. Do you have the fabric you need?" He wasn't sure if the general store was open on Sundays, but he was sure he could find someone to barter with if it became necessary.

Hannah nodded. "Mother and I packed a couple of bolts of cloth for me to use for whatever I needed when we arrived in Oregon. I'll make it so full no one will know the difference. I promise!"

Mary grinned. "You *do* have the best of all husbands, don't you? Now I'm a little upset that you married him before I had a chance."

Hannah knew her friend was only joking, but after what Jed had told her about considering courting Mary, she wasn't altogether pleased by the statement. "Yup, I married him first, so you don't get a chance," Hannah said with a forced smile.

"I thought maybe you'd like to walk today. We could try

to get another deer for supper. We fed four families last night, one of them being mine."

"And your family is huge!" Hannah said. "I really can't though. We're having supper with my mother, and she'll expect us there a little early. I need time to say goodbye."

"Then just go for a walk with me. We'll leave my musket in camp. I think all the others want to tell your husband how wonderful his sermon was, but they don't want to interrupt the newlyweds."

Hannah glanced at Jed who nodded. "Go on. You need to have fun today, while you can."

Hannah leaned down and kissed Jed's forehead. "Thank you for being the kindest of all the husbands in all the land."

He laughed. "You won't be saying that when we're both tired and grumpy from months on the trail."

Hannah hurried off with Mary, and the two of them walked toward the Trail. "I always feel drawn to it. I was fascinated by it even before I knew I was going. I hated the idea of the work involved, of course, but I felt like it was my destiny." She'd taken long walks out to the Trail with her parents before her father had died.

"Really? I feel drawn to it as well, but only because I plan to find my own homestead on the other end of it. Did you tell Jed my plans?"

Hannah shook her head. "I decided that was a secret for just the two of us. We don't have to share it with anyone else until you file the deed."

"Sounds good to me. I feel like I'm encouraging you to lie to your husband, though."

"There's no lie involved. I didn't tell him you weren't getting your own land once we reach Oregon." Hannah shrugged, refusing to worry about it.

"That's true..."

Hannah smiled. "I'm excited to see my mother today. Do you know I've never gone so long without spending time with her? Is that crazy?"

Mary shook her head. "No. I'm the same way. But I'm not saying goodbye. I'll see her every day as we trudge toward Oregon." Mary stopped and stooped down, looking at something. "Deer tracks. Makes me wish I'd brought my musket after all."

Hannah smiled. "I would have been all for it, but I don't want to have to change clothes, and yesterday, we got some blood on my dress."

"Would that frighten your mother?" Mary asked. "My ma is used to me coming home covered in blood and mud and all kinds of other things."

"Yes, but I think you've had a lot more freedom in your life than I have. It was good while my father was alive, but when my mother remarried, things weren't the same. My step-father really expected me to act like a lady at all times, and he made it clear that if I didn't, I would bring shame upon his household."

"He sounds like a real...well the word I want to say might get me struck by lightning." Mary grinned. "Ma said I need to watch my language around the preacher's wife anyway. She thinks that you're uptight or something. She needs to get to know you so she understands there's no need to worry."

Hannah nodded. "I'd like to get to know her as well. I'm not one of those women who is offended by everything. I should probably get offended a little more often than I do."

"Well, don't just yet. I want my friend first." Mary stopped beside a tree. "See this? The deer rub their horns on trees."

"Oh, really? That's what this is? I'm learning so much from you. Surely there's something I can teach you."

"You can teach me how to pretend to be a lady," Mary answered quickly. "Ma thinks you're a good example for me. She doesn't understand that I'm working hard at bringing you down to my level."

Hannah laughed. "What she doesn't know won't hurt her, will it?"

They walked and talked a good long while before finally walking back to Jed's wagon. When he wasn't there, Hannah frowned. "He didn't say anything about going anywhere."

Mary shrugged. "Let's ask around."

They went from wagon to wagon, asking everyone if they'd seen the preacher. By the time they got to the fifth wagon, that of Margaret Bolling—a young widow with two daughters—they spotted him coming toward them. Rather than running toward her husband as she wanted to do, Hannah made small talk with Margaret.

"I'm hoping I can get some meat by offering to cook for some of the bachelors on the Trail," Margaret said. "I can't hunt, but I sure can cook."

"I'll pass the word along to others," Hannah said automatically. "Mary is a good hunter, and she may be able to help you with meat as well."

"Well, that would be right kind of you, Miss Mitchell." Margaret smiled at Mary, her eyes pleading for help.

Hannah's heart went out to the woman. She couldn't imagine losing Jed at such a young age. Why, Mrs. Bolling couldn't be more than two or three years older than she was.

Mary smiled. "Any extras will go straight to your pot. I will try to get you at least a small animal every day."

"Thank you," Mrs. Bolling said, breathing a sigh of

relief. "Now I don't have to be quite as nervous about this journey."

Hannah smiled. "You have friends in us. We'll help any way we can." She looked at Mary. "I'm heading over to see what Jed's been up to. He usually lets me know if he's leaving."

"That sounds good. I'm heading back to my family. I might see if I can get a deer for supper and to make jerky out of. I know where to bring any extras now." Mary smiled at Mrs. Bolling who smiled back.

"The girls and I would be very grateful. They're sleeping now, or they'd tell you themselves."

Hannah felt even worse for Mrs. Bolling at that moment, realizing she wouldn't be able to walk with the rest of them. Instead, she'd be driving her own wagon. What a difficult thing for a widow to do, but Hannah had only respect for her.

When she got back to her own wagon, she looked at Jed curiously. "You didn't say you were going anywhere."

"I had to find you a wedding present. And a 'we're leaving tomorrow' present." He smiled. "Or maybe two presents."

Hannah frowned. "You didn't need to get me a present."

"You've been such a good sport so far, making it clear that you don't think you're above sleeping under the stars or walking beside a wagon. I wanted to get you something. Hold out your hands and close your eyes."

Hannah obeyed, but she felt silly doing it. When she had a small fluffy, squirming ball of life pressed into each hand, she squealed. "Kittens? Really?"

He grinned. "I got you a tom and a female. They're from different litters, so we can breed them for more."

She stared at the cute little kittens, who couldn't have been weaned for long. "They're perfect. Which is which?"

"The tom is black, and the girl is the tabby."

"Oh, they're going to be a huge responsibility on the Trail, but I don't even care. My very own kittens!" After snuggling them both under her chin for a moment, she carefully set the two small critters down and threw her arms around her husband. "Thank you." She raised her face and kissed him, surprising him and herself.

Jed smiled. "I'm glad you like the present. When you told me about having to give away Mr. Whiskers, I just knew I needed to get you a kitten or two. Just don't name them anything silly," he said.

"So, Mr. and Mrs. Whiskers would be bad?" she asked, smiling sweetly.

"Yes, that would be *very* bad."

"I think I'll name them Frederick and Fredericka. I'll call the tom Freddie and the girl Ricka."

He groaned. "If you have to."

"Oh, I certainly do!" She sat down on the ground with the two kittens who were rolling around biting one another. "Now you two are going to stop fighting and fall in love, all right?"

Jed considered explaining about kitten biology for a moment, but decided against it. If she wanted to believe they had to love each other to make babies, then she could believe that all day long.

"Who's going to watch them while we're at my parents for supper? We can't take them."

"Do you think Miss Mitchell would mind?" he asked.

"I'm sure she wouldn't! I'll go ask her right now." She had taken to wearing an apron around the camp, and she had two pockets. One kitten went into each pocket as she ran off to show Mary.

Her friend had just put her musket over her shoulder when she arrived. "Oh, I forgot you were hunting. I was hoping you could watch my kittens."

Mary laughed. "Go ask Mrs. Bolling. I'm sure her girls will love to play with them." She shook her head. "I can't believe you're taking kittens on the trail."

"Me neither!" Hannah hurried off to Mrs. Bolling, explaining the situation. "Would you and your girls be willing to mind the kittens while I'm at my parents' house for supper?"

Mrs. Bolling smiled and reached for the kittens. "We would be happy to. Amanda? Sally? Come see the kittens."

Two little blond girls climbed down out of the wagon and approached the kittens. Satisfied her babies were in good hands, Hannah went back to Jed. "Can we walk into town?" she asked. "I need to build up my muscles as quickly as possible." She was already sore from all the walking she'd done, but she didn't care. She was going to be a pioneer in one more day, and she had to prepare for it. Hopefully her muscles would build up enough that she wouldn't constantly be sore as they travelled.

Jed smiled and nodded, and the two struck out toward town. "I'm glad you like the kittens."

"Like? I love them. Thank you so much for thinking of them. They're just the distraction I'll need on the Trail." She hesitated for a moment, but then told him what Margaret Bolling had said about being willing to cook in exchange for meat in her pot. "I'm afraid they won't be able to make it all the way to Oregon if they don't get some help."

Jed nodded. "Thanks for letting me know. I'll talk to the

single men that are part of this train. There aren't a lot of them, so it won't be hard to do."

"Good. I think I'll try to walk with her girls during the day, because she'll be driving her wagon."

"We'll all find ways to help," Jed told her. "That's why a group of us go together."

"Good. I don't want to have to worry about her the whole way there." They had arrived at her mother's house, and she walked in, calling out. "Mother, we're here."

Her mother came running out of the parlor and flung her arms around Hannah. "Do you realize this may be the very last time we ever see each other?"

Hannah frowned. "I hadn't thought of it that way, but you're right. It might be." She didn't let herself cry, but she was deeply saddened. "We're going to write to each other, and you will always be welcome in my home in Oregon."

"I don't see Mr. Gatlin and myself traveling the Oregon Trail anytime soon." The sadness in her mother's eyes compounded Hannah's own feelings greatly.

"I suppose not." Hannah smiled. "Tonight is going to be a happy memory for both of us. We're not going to be weeping and worrying about the trip. Instead, we're going to be two women enjoying one another's company."

Over supper, they sat together, and each of them talked about silly things they had done. It was a beautiful trip down memory lane for each of them.

Hannah could see Mr. Gatlin talking to Jed, who simply nodded constantly. She didn't once hear him say a thing.

When the evening was over, Hannah wrapped her arms around her mother and held on tight. "I promise I will write often. You don't have to worry about me, Mother."

Mother sniffled back a tear. "I promised myself I wouldn't cry tonight." She dashed her tear away quickly.

"I want to remember you with smiles, not with tears. You know how much I love to write. I will be putting pen to paper often on this journey of ours, and I'll send you a letter from every fort." Hannah wasn't sure she'd have the time to do so, but she would find it. Her mother was too important to her not to.

"I'll try to have letters waiting for you at those forts," her mother responded.

With a last embrace, Hannah and Jed were gone, walking through the quiet town to return to the campsite. "Are we really ready for this journey?" Hannah asked, looking back over her shoulder only once. It was a good thing her husband wasn't Lot, and she wasn't turned into a pillar of salt, but she couldn't leave without that last glance backward. She now understood what had happened with the other woman, not wanting to leave everything behind.

"We are ready. Tomorrow is the day I've been working toward for months. It's the day we strike out for land of our own, and a congregation that I can teach. We're going to Oregon."

Hannah smiled a little, not missing his enthusiasm. "It's going to be hard, but the rewards will be worth it."

"That's my wife. You know you can do it. We'll do it all together." He took her hand and brought it to his lips, and all at once, she wished they'd had a normal wedding night. She knew neither of them would want to wait much longer before they engaged in the marital act, and she didn't really want to have to try to find a private place on the Trail.

SIX

WE LEFT FOR OREGON TODAY, *and it was a hard day to say the least. My dear bride is sore and tired, but she kept her spirits up and cooked supper for me just as agreed upon. We had to cross the Missouri River this morning, and it was much simpler than expected. We were ferried across the river, and we stayed close, walking along the banks of the river and setting up camp here after a ten-mile drive. All of the wagons are in a circle, and we are all encamped within the circle.*

Hannah spent the first day on the trail walking with Mary and her siblings, whom she was watching over, and watching over Mrs. Bolling's daughters. The girls were excited to start the journey but once they'd had lunch, which was only about a mile after everyone was ferried across the Missouri River, they became cantankerous.

They didn't like to use a hole in the ground to do their business. They didn't like it any better when all the women stood in a circle around them with their skirts spread to keep anyone from seeing them when they went. They really didn't like having to use a leaf to get the feces off their bodies when they were finished. All in all, they were not happy with their first day on the trail.

Hannah suggested to Mrs. Bolling that both of her daughters would do well with a nap in the wagon, and with the other woman's agreement, she lifted both girls in. Once they were settled, Hannah moved back and walked with Mary, whose mother was now there. It was Hannah's first opportunity to meet Mrs. Mitchell.

"It's so good to meet you, Mrs. Mitchell. I truly enjoy Mary's companionship."

Mrs. Mitchell shook her head. "Just make sure she learns your *good* habits, and you don't learn her bad ones."

Hannah couldn't help the laugh that escaped her. "I'm not learning anything from Mary that my husband doesn't approve of." It was true, but she knew Mrs. Mitchell probably wouldn't be as lenient with her as Jed was.

As they walked, Hannah had the kittens in her pockets some, and sometimes let them down to walk. Without fail, they would start rolling around and biting one another within minutes of being put on the ground, and Hannah would grumble and carry them again. She honestly wasn't sure which would hurt her arms more, carrying the kittens or driving the wagon.

The day, she was told, would be like most days on the trail. They'd been woken up by a shot into the sky, and they'd had a short while to have breakfast, make coffee, take care of their bodily needs, and get their wagons reloaded for the day's drive. Then they'd crossed the river and started walking.

By the end of that first day, Hannah was certain she would never be able to move again, but she was careful not to complain. What was the use? Everyone else would have been hurting as well. Maybe not everyone else had been raised without much exercise, but they would still be sore.

She thought longingly of her bed back in Independence and her bath that would be filled twice a week with warm water and would magically be taken away when she was finished, the water dumped out, and the tub cleaned for when she was next ready for a bath.

Mary didn't seem at all bothered as she walked with her rifle thrown over one shoulder, and she shot three rabbits. She quickly gave one to Mrs. Bolling, and the other two she claimed as supper for her family.

"Mary, I never know if I should be pleased that you provide meat or scold you because you do it in the manliest way possible!" her mother said.

Mary grinned. "Just be happy I provide meat, of course."

Just before they stopped for the day, Mary hit one more rabbit, and she gave it to Hannah. "I'll show you how to skin it when we stop. My brother can do the ones for my family."

Hannah nodded, feeling tired and a bit overwhelmed. What had she been thinking that she could do this? She'd walked all day, and now she was expected to cook supper. It was going to be a very long six months. She already felt ready to drop to the ground and get someone—anyone—to return her to the home where she belonged.

When they finally camped for the evening, Hannah followed Mary, and she learned how to skin a rabbit. Mary was a good teacher, telling her what to do but making Hannah do it.

Hannah followed every step her friend told her to make, even though the thought of cooking something that had been hopping through the fields just moments before turned her stomach.

When the animal had been skinned, Hannah stared at it. "How do I cook a rabbit?" She wasn't sure she even knew people ate rabbit until that moment. Rabbits were sweet little creatures you fed and watched as they played happily.

"You've never had rabbit?" Mary asked.

Hannah shook her head. "No, never."

"Make a stew out of it. Now I wouldn't remove the meat from the bones. Just let the preacher know that's how you cooked it, so he knows to watch out for bones. You should have enough for a good noonday meal tomorrow as well. Make some biscuits with it, and you have breakfast, a noonday meal, and tonight's supper all at once."

Hannah nodded. "Are you sore at all from the walking?" She needed to rub the knots out of her legs, but she didn't want to do it in front of her friend.

Mary shook her head with a grin. "I walked five miles each way to school. Walking is easy."

"I'll be as strong as you in a few days, won't I?" Hannah could hear the pleading tone of her own voice, and she knew she was being silly, but she was so sore, she wasn't sure she could keep going.

"You will. I promise."

They parted ways, and Hannah realized that Mrs. Bolling had her wagon parked right next to hers and Jed's. She'd make sure to help the other woman all she could.

Jed was off somewhere with the livestock, and she collected some wood for supper. She knew there was a bit in the wagon, but Jed had said that was for further down the road when wood wouldn't be readily available. Here it was easy to find, some big logs had even been left behind by other caravans, though Hannah was relatively certain their train was the first of the year.

She made the fire, and then she cut up the rabbit as best she could. The kittens played at her feet as she did, and she was happy they hadn't wandered off. They seemed to know she was their protector, and they needed to stay with her.

The stew took a couple of hours to cook, and her mouth was watering most of that time. She could smell how good the stew would be. There were few spices to be had, but she made do, and when she served Jed his meal, he smiled. "This is really good."

"I think so too. Are you wanting to play cards with other couples again tonight?" she asked.

He shook his head. "Not tonight. I think everyone's too tired to think about cards or music or anything. Once we're more used to the daily chores of being on the Trail, we'll all do better with it."

"I certainly hope you're right." Already, it felt as if her enthusiasm was gone. She wanted to turn tail and go home, but that wasn't the answer. No, she would have to be strong and just handle it all.

She wrapped the biscuits for breakfast the following day in a piece of cloth, and then she left the stew right in the pot and covered it. It was cold enough at night that there was no worry about the food spoiling.

She spooned out a portion of the stew and put it in a bowl for the kittens to share, and then she added a small bit of milk to another bowl. The kittens lapped it up happily. She'd decided to feed them a little of their supper and some milk every day until they started hunting for their own food.

She washed the few dishes they'd used right in the river, and carried them back up to the wagon. The sun was setting, but it was still early. "Would I seem like a sloth if I went to bed now?"

Jed laughed. "Look around you."

It seemed that most people had been exhausted from the day's work and decided to sleep early as well. With as cold as it was, it took more energy to do most things. The tents had all been erected with a few of the unmarried men sleeping outside in a bedroll.

She smiled. "I think I'm going to write in my journal very quickly and then follow suit. Today was long and hard, but tomorrow will be just like today." She nodded toward the tent he'd set up while she was cooking supper. "Thanks for making sure we had shelter."

"We'll leave the river tomorrow and head for Mosquito Creek, which *shouldn't* be covered in mosquitoes," he said with a smile. "We always want to camp on water when we can, because we'll need it. The barrel of water in the wagon is never to be used for anything but cooking. All right?"

"That makes sense to me." She covered a yawn with her hand. Climbing into the wagon, she lit a small lantern and quickly wrote in her journal about her day. She talked about the time with Mary and her mother, and watching Mrs. Bolling's girls, and skinning her first rabbit. She was sure there would be many more to come. As soon as she'd finished, she turned down the lantern and stowed her journal back in her trunk.

Gathering the bedding she and Jed would share, she took it outside and laid one blanket on the ground of the tent, and left the other three to cover them. When they snuggled closely together, it provided enough warmth that they made it through the night. She wondered what would have happened to him without her body heat.

Once they were bedded down for the night, she said a

silent prayer, thanking God for getting them to their first destination safely. There would be many more destinations and many more days to travel, but they would take those one day at a time.

————

HANNAH WOKE AGAIN to the sound of the gunshot, and for just a moment, she snuggled under the covers closer to her husband. "I want to stay in bed all day," she said softly.

He wrapped an arm around her and held her close. "I would too, but it's time for work." He yawned right in her ear, and she sat up.

"I'll get the fire started," she said with another yawn, doing her best to force herself to wake up.

"I'll go help make sure the livestock didn't wander too far during the night." He sat up, pulling his suspenders over his shoulders. He went to the wagon, and drew on his heavy coat and went to join the other men, while Hannah started the fire for their coffee.

By the time he got back to camp, she had the coffee made, and she had even melted butter on their biscuits and added jam. He sat down on the ground beside her, still yawning. "Two of the Jensen's cows wandered off during the night. I got them, and they're back where they belong."

"Good. We'll need all of our livestock when we get to Oregon." Hannah handed him his cup of coffee and his plate of biscuits and jam. "How far do you think we'll go today?"

"The goal is always twenty miles per day. Whether we can do that is a completely different story. We did ten yesterday, but it took almost half the day to get the wagons ferried across the water."

"I will do everything I can to keep up." She sighed. "I don't think I told you I have new names for the kittens."

"Oh? What did you decide on?" He hoped it wasn't one of her silly names for the animals.

"I named the girl Naughty."

He laughed. "And the tom is Nice?" he asked, grinning.

"Oh, no. The tom is Naughtier."

"Now *those* are good names for those two." He poured a little cream from the milk bucket out into a saucer for the kittens, and they both gobbled it up greedily.

A short while later, they were ready to move on. Hannah walked with Amanda and Sally, holding their hands and talking to them. She pointed out any animals she saw and any other things she could think of that might be of interest to two little girls.

Mary walked beside her, musket at the ready. "I'm going to try for a deer today. That would be enough food for all three families and more."

"You've taken it upon yourself to feed Mrs. Bolling's family every night, haven't you?" Hannah asked.

"Of course, I have. Just because I carry a musket doesn't mean I don't have a soft heart." Mary looked past Hannah. "Jeremiah, get out of those weeds. We follow the trail for a reason!"

A small boy, who couldn't have been more than five, hurried over to Mary. "Sorry, Mary. I thought I saw a snake."

Mary closed her eyes for a moment. "If you see a snake, it could be poisonous. We don't want to bury you in Iowa now, do we?" She pointed to a human skull on the ground not too far off the trail.

"No. I guess not. I'm going to run up ahead and see what the wagons are doing."

Mary shook her head at Hannah. "He's the most curious boy I've ever met. He constantly needs to be learning new things and seeing new things. He's going to be dead by the time we reach Nebraska. Ma took half the children today, just so I could keep a better eye on Jeremiah."

Hannah shook her head, glad the girls were being so cooperative. At the moment, at least. "It's strange to see so much barren land after being on the banks of the Missouri so long. Jed said we're looking to camp on Mosquito Creek tonight. It sounds itchy to me."

"Me too. I guess that's one of the benefits of traveling when it's colder than a witch's tit. Not as many bugs around to bite us."

Hannah giggled at the crude expression. "Well, I'm glad we won't be eaten alive by bugs at least. Not until it warms up some anyway."

"Do you know if we're stopping for the noon meal today?" Mary asked.

"Why wouldn't we?" Hannah asked. "Won't we stop for a noon meal every day?" If they were going to walk all day every day, then they needed to stop for food in her opinion. How else would they have the energy to keep going?

"Probably not. We're trying to make really good time to beat the winter to Oregon. I'm not sure if it's even possible, but I know the men have been talking about it since we all camped together in Independence."

"Doesn't Independence feel forever away now? I lived there my whole life until yesterday, and now it seems almost as if it's just a distant memory."

Mary nodded. "It does feel that way. It feels like the only real people in the whole world are the ones on this journey with us. Will we even remember how to talk to people when we get there?"

"I hope we will," Hannah said. "I'm a preacher's wife, after all, and I'm going to have to act all proper after the trail. Jed is fine with a split skirt for now, but I can tell you with a certainty that he is going to expect me to act like a lady after we arrive in Oregon."

"He probably *will* expect it. And I'll be off on my homestead wearing trousers and shooting at any critter I see." Mary grinned. "We'll have to enjoy being equals while we're on the trail, because we certainly weren't before, and we won't be after."

"We'll always be equals, because we'll always be women working as hard as we can toward a goal. Now if one of us lazed about and did nothing, then she would be inferior. There is absolutely *nothing* inferior about you, Mary Mitchell."

Mary grinned. "I guess not." She stopped walking and brought her musket to her shoulder and shot off into the distance. She raised a hand in victory as the buck she was shooting at fell. "I got him. We have supper! Keep going. I'll catch up."

Hannah didn't see what other choice she had, so she and the girls continued walking alongside the wagons. They stopped a short while later for the noon meal, and after returning the girls to their mother, Hannah stretched out her legs as she put cold stew into two bowls, taking both to Jed on the wagon. She climbed up beside him and ate a few bites of stew. It certainly wasn't as good cold as it was warm, but it was palatable.

"Mary just shot a deer. She plans to feed half the camp with it tonight," Hannah said with a smile. "I've never seen anyone handle a gun the way she does."

"She really is skilled," Jed agreed.

"How are things going today?" she asked. "Are we making good time?"

"We are. We should be at Mosquito Creek after another couple of hours of travel, and we'll spend the night there."

"And what's the next thing we'll reach after that?" She knew Jed had a map that he was constantly referring to that told him where they were going and what landmarks they'd see first.

"Wolf River is where we'll head tomorrow. We'll need to use rafts to cross that river from what I understand."

"We'll have wood and water, then. That's what we're looking for every night, isn't it?"

Jed nodded with a smile. "That's exactly what we're looking for every night. There'll be a lot of nights we have to use buffalo chips to cook with or to warm ourselves by, but one of those nights will *not* be tonight."

Hannah wrinkled her nose. "I suppose it'll be my job to collect them?"

He grinned. "You are the one who needs a fire to cook, after all."

"You need a wife to cook for you...maybe you could help her out with the buffalo chips."

"We'll see." He kissed her as she hopped down. The gunshot had sounded. "It's time for our afternoon walk."

"You make it sound a great deal more leisurely than it really is."

"Are you complaining?" he asked.

"How can I complain when there are people who have it so much harder than we do?" She couldn't get Mrs. Bolling out of her mind. Her job was so much harder than Hannah's was.

"That's a very good attitude."

Hannah nodded, smiling at him as she headed toward

the Bolling wagon. "Do you want me to walk with the girls?" she asked.

Mrs. Bolling shook her head. "No, I think they're ready for their nap. Your help is greatly appreciated, though."

"Mary shot a deer for supper, so you don't have to worry about an empty pot tonight."

"What would we do without sweet Miss Mitchell?"

"Survive on biscuits and beans, most likely," Hannah said. "I'll check on you in an hour or two."

"Thank you."

Hannah walked back to Mary, who was again accompanied by her mother. "Mrs. Mitchell, it's good to see you out and about this afternoon."

"I was out this morning as well, but I was walking on the other side of the wagons," Mrs. Mitchell responded. "It's easier to keep some of my younger boys from causing mischief if they're apart."

"Sounds like a good plan then." Hannah felt the kittens getting restless, so she put them down to walk again, watching them closely. "I think Naughty and Naughtier are ready for a little bit of walking as well. I've had them in my pockets all morning."

Mary grinned. "I'm sure they're ready to be free for a little while." Both friends loved to watch the kittens exploring their new reality every day.

"I just worry one of them will be hurt by a wild animal," Hannah said, watching as they ran beside one of the wagons for a bit. "I don't want anything to happen to them."

"Of course not," Mary said. "They're so sweet!" Mary spotted something Hannah couldn't see. "Ma, the twins are rolling in the dirt fighting again. Jeremiah!"

Mrs. Mitchell groaned. "Jesse!" She looked at Mary.

"We'll split up again. I think I'll go walk with Mrs. Bedwell. She tries to keep her boys separated as well."

After Mrs. Mitchell was gone, Hannah watched Mary slouch a little and she immediately looked more like the Mary Hannah was used to. "You make me laugh," Hannah said. "You act all proper around your mother, but when it's just the two of us, you seem to turn into someone else."

"You're right. I turn into the *real* Mary as soon as Ma turns her back." Mary shook her head. "I hate having to act one way for Ma and another way for everyone else. It makes me feel like a hypocrite."

"I can understand that," Hannah said. "I wish there was something you could do."

"Eventually there will be. I just have a few more months of being under Ma's thumb, and then I'll be free to do what I want."

"I'm glad there's an end in sight."

When they reached their campsite on the Mosquito Creek, Hannah immediately gathered her firewood. She wasn't about to get up again after she sat. She even grabbed a bucketful of water for the few dishes. She wondered if she could get Jed to rub her feet. She'd happily return the favor by rubbing his. Of course, his probably didn't hurt like hers did. He was spending his days in the wagon.

When Jed joined her after dealing with his own chores for the evening, she was frying up venison steaks. Mary's deer had once again fed much of the camp, and they hadn't had to get into their store of beans for supper. Hannah was pleased because she didn't particularly enjoy eating beans.

Jed collapsed on the ground beside her, rubbing his upper arms. "One more day behind us. Only about one hundred seventy-eight left."

Hannah groaned. *"Why* would you tell me that?"

"I'm counting down. I want to cheer you up."

She shook her head. "You will not be able to cheer me up until you can tell me there are two days to go."

He laughed. "Supper smells good."

"Thank you. The steaks will be ready in about twenty minutes."

He nodded. "Did we drink all the coffee?"

"We did. Would you like me to make another pot?"

"That would be nice if you don't mind. I don't usually drink coffee with supper, but I feel like it's the best option." He blinked a few times, trying to get the sight of the prairie out of his vision.

"Our next stop is Wolf River, right?" she asked. It made her feel better to always know what their goal was. It made the time go faster somehow.

"It is. We should be there by this time tomorrow, and we'll camp on the river, and then cross over in the morning. It'll probably be a hard day."

Hannah shrugged. "Better to have fewer hard days than more easy ones. We want to be settled by winter, and that means we have to go as quickly as we can, right?"

"Exactly. It depends how high the Wolf River is if we can cross it with rafts or if we'll have to make canoes. We're all hoping the rafts will be enough. They're left from one caravan to the next. Someone has to go over and get them, but that's better than building new ones."

"What do you think? Will the water be low enough?" she asked, slightly worried that the water would be high and they would lose precious travel time.

"I think we'll be able to use the rafts. It doesn't look like rain and all of the creeks and rivers have been low so far. We should make it with ease."

"Oh good. Then we won't lose time."

"You're anxious to be there, aren't you?"

She shrugged. "I'm anxious to be there before winter. We don't need snow impeding us when we build our new house, or when we build the church."

"Very true. How's your split skirt coming?" he asked.

She sighed. "I haven't sewn a stitch. Between the Bolling girls and the kittens, my mind is on anything but my clothing."

"Maybe you can do some work on it on Sunday. We plan to take a day of rest for us as much as for the animals. And for the laundry."

She groaned. "I am not sure I'm ready for laundry on the trail."

"There's really no choice..."

"I know. I'll do it, and I won't complain."

"You are a good wife to me, Hannah."

"Thank you. I'm trying hard."

"It shows."

Hannah wrote in her journal again before bed. It was time for them to reach Wolf River. They were going to keep moving along the Trail no matter what.

SEVEN

THE DAYS ARE SO LONG, *and the nights are much too short. Today was our third day on the Trail, and I'm already exhausted and want to cry with how much I ache in every bone of my body.*

Mary Mitchell's brother managed to shoot himself in the foot with her musket today. Thank heavens we have a doctor traveling with our train, and he came to the rescue, patching up Jeremiah. The child has been into everything since before we started on the trail, so I'm certain he will heal well and will be up and about soon—and back into making as much mischief as he can.

We are camped on the Wolf River tonight, and we expect to be able to cross in the morning on rafts that were found on the river. Bob Hastings volunteered to swim across the river to retrieve the rafts. He is a brave soul, to be willing to swim through that icy water to help the rest of us. We had a fire ready for him along with many blankets when he returned.

Hopefully, he will be up to helping us all cross the river in the morning, but even if he isn't, he has made it possible for all of us to cross the river, and it will probably take another half day. My aching feet make me pleased we are spending the morning crossing tomorrow, and there will be no walking. I'm certain I'll regret saying this in the morning, but for now, it is the truth.

Wednesday was another long, hard day for Hannah and the rest of the emigrants. They had lost their early excitement for the journey and now were dealing with the daily drudgery of the Trail.

Hannah walked beside Mary, who had her musket on her shoulder throughout the morning as always. They chattered about their lives before the Trail, and Amanda and Sally walked alongside them a little more cheerfully that day.

"You girls seem very happy today," Hannah finally said. "Did something happen?"

Amanda, the older of the girls, shrugged. "No, but we like seeing the animals."

"The animals do bring joy, don't they?" Hannah said with a smile.

Little Sally nodded her head. "I love the kitties."

Hannah looked around her. She hadn't thought of her kittens for a few minutes, and she worried they may have left them, but they were following along, hoping for the food they knew Hannah had for them.

When the train stopped for the noon meal, Hannah went to their wagon and got out food she'd cooked the night before, splitting it into two bowls and carrying half to Jed. Just as she was settling herself on the wagon seat beside him, she heard a gunshot.

Assuming a member of the party had gotten an animal for supper, she smiled. "Someone will have meat tonight."

Then there was a scream from behind them, and Jed all but leapt off the seat and ran back. He found Jeremiah Mitchell lying on the ground with blood pouring from his foot. "Doc!" he yelled as loudly as he could. "Did you shoot yourself in the foot?" He wanted to call him a fool boy, but that would do no good with a boy as headstrong as Jeremiah.

The doctor hurried back to Jed and looked at the boy on the ground, shaking his head. "Played with your sister's musket, did you?" The disgust on the doctor's face was clear. They all knew the boy should have been watched more closely.

More and more people gathered around as the doctor went back for his medical bag. Captain Bedwell groaned. "He's going to have to ride after Doc patches him up. We don't need to be slowed down by a fool boy who couldn't keep his hands off a gun." He walked away shaking his head while everyone else worked to make the boy more comfortable. He was not an easy man, and he had no pity for fools. He had a schedule to keep, and by God, they would keep it.

Mr. Mitchell grabbed Mary by the arm and dragged her off, and Hannah could hear his yells coming from wherever he took her, but at least she couldn't quite make out the words he was saying. She felt terrible for her friend, knowing she would blame herself for her brother's accident, and being taken to task right after it happened would only hurt, not help.

Hannah knelt on the ground and grasped Jeremiah's hand while his mother put a pillow under his head. Mrs. Bolling carefully removed the boy's boot. After removing Jeremiah's sock, the doctor poured a good measure of whiskey over the gunshot wound and ignored the boy's screams of intense pain.

Hannah was revolted by the look of his foot as the sock

came off, but she swallowed hard to keep her lunch in her stomach. There would be no time to cook something else if she vomited. The Trail was going to make her a stronger person, or it was going to kill her. There was no other option.

They were slowed down by about an hour by the time they took care of Jeremiah and settled him in the back of one of his parents' wagons and got back on their way, but Jed was optimistic. "We should still be able to get to the Wolf River this afternoon, and we'll be able to camp there. Unless some other fool boy shoots himself or something," he told Hannah, shaking his head. No one was very sympathetic about the accident. Instead, they thought the boy should have had the sense God gave a lizard, and he apparently didn't."

As Hannah walked beside Mary that afternoon, her friend was mostly quiet. The girls were napping, as they always did in the afternoons, and Hannah was worried for Mary. "Are you all right?"

Mary turned to Hannah with tears pouring down her cheeks. "Pa has always told me never to leave my musket sitting around, and this is why. I hurt my brother."

"No, Mary, you didn't. You were a little careless, true, but I'm sure your brother has been told never to touch a musket as well. You can't take all the blame for this. Besides, his foot is mending, and he gets to ride for a few days."

Mary sniffled. "I feel like I should ride with him to take care of him."

"Your mother is riding with him. She'll take good care of him." Hannah hugged her friend for a moment. "He'll be all right."

"What if his foot becomes putrid? What if he dies, and it's all my fault!"

"It won't be. I know your father taught your siblings as well as he taught you, and he wouldn't have let your brother get to be five without teaching him not to play with guns, would he?"

Mary sighed, shaking her head. "Of course not, but he would never have touched it if I hadn't left it laying around loaded, now would he?"

"Of course not. But it's still not your fault. You're going to have to figure out how not to beat yourself up over it. The doctor has taken care of him, and you have to trust that he's going to be just fine." Hannah hoped her words were actually reaching her friend. She didn't know what else to say that would convince her.

"I'll try."

They walked a little later in the day that way, but true to his word, Captain Bedwell got them to the Wolf River late that afternoon. For once, Hannah didn't take the time to worry about all the pain she was in. Instead, she simply got to work making supper. There was no meat that evening, so she made a filling supper of beans and biscuits. It wouldn't have been her first choice of a meal, but it would see them through.

As she ate the beans, she swallowed down her negative feelings about them and reminded herself how thankful she was to have food to cook. It was their first time to get into the bean stores, and they'd already been on the road for three days—though it felt like three weeks. It was very strange how slowly time passed on the Trail. Her time before they'd started the journey felt like it was in the distant past.

Jed helped the others make sure the livestock were rounded up before he joined her. "Right after supper, Bob Hastings is going to swim across the river for the rafts.

Unless there's a sudden downpour tonight, and it doesn't look like there will be, we should have an easy time crossing. We'll go over first thing in the morning and keep traveling along the Wolf River for a few days. We'll have water, meat, and wood for a while yet."

"Tomorrow is only half a day walking then, right?"

He nodded with a smile. "Are your feet still hurting you that badly?" He hated that the trip was causing her pain, but it made sense. It wasn't a picnic for any of them.

"They are. I want to stick them in the river to numb them. Numb would be better than this constant pain I feel."

"I'll rub your feet later after we get the tent set up."

Hannah perked at the idea. "I can't ask you to do that. You've been driving all day, and I would bet your hands and arms are as sore as my feet."

"I'm fine. We could put some liniment on them tonight as well if you'd like."

She shook her head. "I hate the smell of liniment. I'll be trying to escape my own stench if we do that."

He laughed. "I'll just rub them then. It's really no problem."

While the ladies did the supper dishes, all the men went to the river to watch Bob swim across to get to the rafts. He was smart about it, and put the first he saw in the river, before grabbing a stick to float the other raft across in front of him. It looked like he was playing some sort of odd game, but he did a good job of it. When he'd gotten both across, he hurried to the fire closest to the bank.

After that excitement was over, and Jed knew Bob was in good hands, he walked over to Hannah and set up the tent. "I'm guessing you don't want people to see you get a foot massage." They might think she was being pampered by him, and he didn't think either of them wanted that.

"No. I don't want people to think I'm not capable of this journey, because I'm just as capable as anyone else. Do you have any idea how Mrs. Bedwell is doing?" She had barely seen the sickly woman since they'd left Independence.

He shook his head. "She doesn't seem to be walking with the others. She's riding in the wagon with Captain Bedwell today, and the boys are walking and finding *all* the mischief they can."

"Of course, they are! As you would have done at their age." Hannah could see the spark of mischief that was still in his eyes. She hoped he didn't plan to play silly jokes on his congregants.

"Yes, I would have," he said. "I'm not even ashamed of it."

"Nor should you be." She got out their blankets and got them organized, and settled herself on the ground inside the tent.. "Does this work for you?"

He nodded. "You might want to remove your shoes and socks though."

She laughed. "I thought about that, but I wanted to make sure we were all settled for the night first."

"That makes sense." He waited as she removed her socks and shoes. Taking one foot onto his lap, he rubbed the knots that he found. "I'm not sure if I'm doing this right."

"I'm not either, but it feels good so *please* keep going."

He laughed. "What a pair we are."

After he'd finished with her feet, he lay down beside her. "Feel better?"

She nodded. "I'm not sleepy yet though."

"Neither am I." He looked at her, and it was still just a tad bit light out, and he could see her green eyes and her beautiful smile. Without thinking about what he was doing, he leaned toward her and touched his lips to hers lightly.

Hannah had become worried that he didn't find her attractive, so when he kissed her, she turned more fully to him and wrapped her arms around him. She'd been waiting for this kiss, and it was finally happening. She was going to make the most of it.

His arms came around her and he pressed her to him more fully, one of his legs wrapping around hers. His hands began to roam over the front of her, cupping her breast through the thin material of her dress and chemise.

She wound her fingers through his hair, clutching him closer to her.

"Do you want to go for a walk away from everyone?" he whispered, his breathing ragged.

"We'd have to stop to walk away," she complained, not wanting to stop touching and kissing. She clung to him to keep him from moving away from her.

"If we walk away, then we can finish this without worry of being interrupted," he said. He said a silent prayer she'd say yes. When he'd agreed to not consummate the marriage, he'd had no idea what having almost contact with her would do to his body. He needed her to agree to go for that walk. He had never made love, but he had an idea it would not be a quiet thing.

She pulled back and picked up the blanket they'd been lying on to take with them. "Let's go." She wasn't even going to stop to put shoes on.

He grinned, realizing they were finally going to make love. Yes, he knew they'd only been married for a few days, but it felt like much longer with the time they'd spent together.

They walked a short distance from the campsite, and she spread the blanket out close to the river. They'd walked the whole way in silence, hoping no one would realize what they were about to do.

Hannah walked to Jed and wrapped her arms around his neck, kissing him once again. It didn't take long for the feelings of need to come back, and her nipples tightened with the cold and the electricity that was spreading between their bodies.

He cupped her bottom as he kissed her, pulling her close to the place where he needed her the most. "I need to touch your skin..."

Hannah nodded, turning so he could unbutton her dress. When he'd finished, she dropped her dress to the ground, and next came her undergarments. It felt strange to her to be completely naked outside in front of a man, but it felt glorious. She hoped their house in Oregon was far enough from neighbors they could make love outside from time to time.

He stepped to her, kissing her again, touching all of her as he did. Finally, he pushed her down onto the blanket she'd spread. He kissed her neck and then moved his lips down to her nipple, taking one of the tight points into his mouth. "You're beautiful," he mumbled against her breast, as his hands stroked all over her naked body.

His hand went to the spot between her legs where her body ached, and he carefully stroked there, trying to make sure she was ready for him, but he wasn't exactly sure what he was looking for. He was glad his first time was with her, but he wished he could have found a manual on how to do it right.

Finally, he couldn't wait another moment, and he rolled away from her and stood, unbuttoning his shirt as quickly as he knew how. When he dropped his pants, he groaned aloud when his member was freed and no longer constrained by his trousers.

He joined her again on the blanket and kissed her, bringing her back quickly to the fevered state she'd been in before he left her.

When he joined his body with hers, he gasped at the feeling. He held still for a moment, loathe to hurt her.

Her hands roamed over his back, and she sighed. "Are we finished?"

He laughed. "We've barely started, love."

Love. He'd called her love. Through the pain of that first time with him, it was all she could think about. He'd called her love.

It was over much too soon for Jed's tastes, but he pulled her close to him as the cold wind dried the sweat on their bodies. Neither spoke for a long while, but finally, Hannah whispered, "I'm getting too cold. We need to get back to camp where the other blankets are."

He kissed her once again. "Thank you."

She laughed. "Why are you thanking me? It was my marital duty, and if I'm honest, it felt good." Hannah thought back to the talk her mother had with her about what the marital act was like, and she found she'd had no desire to plan meals in her head. It was so much more fun to feel everything that was happening.

He caught her lips one last time. "Let's get dressed and get back to camp."

"Maybe we should start pitching our tent far away from the others."

He shook his head. "No, we'll just sneak away whenever we want to."

He reached down a hand and helped her to her feet, and they quickly dressed. Hannah didn't bother with the buttons on the back of her dress when she was just going to sleep anyway.

When they got back to the tent, they smoothed out the blanket together and shared their sleeping space, sleeping in one another's arms. Just before she fell asleep, she remembered her journal entry for the day, but she decided she would write it in the morning as if she'd written it then. She really didn't want to skip a day writing, but lying in her husband's arms was infinitely more important at the moment.

The following morning, the first thing Hannah did was scramble for her journal and write down her thoughts, carefully omitting the events of the night before. She certainly didn't want her grandchildren reading about the first time she'd made love with their preacher grandfather.

The shot still hadn't sounded when she was finished, so she moved to the spot where she'd started a fire the night before. The morning at least would be spent in trying to raft all the wagons across the river, and she knew she wouldn't be walking nearly as much, which was good because she was now sore in new places.

She started the fire and got a pot of coffee going, and then packed up as much as she could of their camp. Jed emerged at the sound of the gunshot into the sky as he did every morning, but the first thing he did was walk around behind Hannah and wrap his arms around her, resting his cheek atop her head. "Good morning, love."

She felt herself melting back against him. "I thought I'd cook a real breakfast this morning since I woke early." And when he called her love, her heart beat faster. How had she not known the instant she saw him that he would be the man she would love for the rest of her days?

"And what is in this real breakfast?" he asked.

"Flapjacks."

"That sounds delicious. If you look carefully, there is some maple syrup back there. I know we'll both want the sugary sweetness of that to add to our days."

She laughed, turning to face him. "I told Mary once you were the very best of all husbands, and I see now that I didn't exaggerate even a little bit. You truly are the best of all husbands."

He leaned down and kissed her. "I need to go help round up the livestock and get ready for our turn to cross the river. Once everything is readied, I'll come back and eat with you. Lots of coffee!" he called over his shoulder as he went to help the men. Someone had suggested keeping the livestock penned in the midst of their wagon circle, but Captain Bedwell hadn't liked the idea. He wished the man would be more bending in things they could decide as a community.

True to his word, Jed was back as she finished making his pancakes. She put a dab of butter on them and then added the syrup, which she had to find in their food storage. Pouring him a cup of coffee, she handed him both, and put a bit of the milk he brought her into a bowl for the kittens.

He talked of rafting the wagons across the stream with her, and it was obvious he was a little worried about how to do it. "The oxen are well-trained, but I'm not exactly a well-trained oxen driver." He shook his head. "They should make you take a class to learn to drive before they let you loose on the Trail.

She smiled. "I haven't seen you try to do anything you weren't excellent at doing. That either means you have practiced doing many things, and you will only do those things you are already good at, or you are naturally good at most things. Which is it?"

He laughed. "You give me confidence."

"I'm glad. We've only been on the trail for four days, so it's nice if you still have confidence."

"And we've been married six days. Tomorrow will make seven. Are you ready to be married for a week?"

"I think I've liked the past twelve hours of marriage more than any other," she answered honestly. Though she hadn't enjoyed the marriage act quite as much as he had, she had loved how close she felt to him. She loved lying in his arms afterward. All-in-all, it felt good to her.

"Glad to hear it. We may have to have a repeat of last night's activities soon."

She had packed everything but the coffee pot, and the plates they were eating on, when the men gathered to try to get the first wagon across the river. First, they loaded Captain Bedwell's wagon onto a raft and floated it across, and when that went well, they began with the other wagons.

Without an experienced ferry man this crossing took much longer than the last had, and they worked well into the afternoon getting all the wagons and all of the pioneers across onto the other side of the river.

They didn't take a break for the noon meal, because the captain was determined to be able to continue along the trail that day, and the women watched with worried expressions as their men went much longer than usual without food. Finally, when she could stand it no more, Hannah took a bowl of cold beans to her husband, and she watched as many of the other women followed suit. The men ate standing up, and they took turns at it, but they ate.

At just before four that afternoon, all of the wagons were across the river, but it was really time to stop for the day. They set up camp in the spot where they could see many others before them had camped across the river from where they'd stayed the previous night.

There was a skeleton of a baby not far from the campsite that some of the children found, and there were marks on one of the legs where a wolf had obviously gnawed at it. Hannah couldn't help but shed a few tears for the mother who had lost her child in some horrific fashion.

At that moment she grew slightly morose, looking around her and wondering which of the people she'd already grown to call her friends would die. For one out of every five who set out for Oregon never arrived.

EIGHT

April first, 1852

WE SPENT all day doing our best to make it across the Wolf River. Finally, late this afternoon, we floated the last wagon across the river. Tonight, we will camp across the river from the place we camped last night, and tomorrow we will travel along the river.

While we men worked to get the wagons across the river, Miss Mitchell shot two deer and two antelopes. That will feed the train for the night, and we will all share in the bounty. I have a feeling she is supplying a great many people with the food they need for the journey, but I have not yet had this confirmed. I do know she has fed us a few nights, and I will give her powder and balls to make up for what she has used to help us.

So far, our journey has been much easier than expected, and I thank God for that hourly. He is providing for us in an amazing way. I continue to ask for His blessing to get us to Oregon in one piece.

That evening was festive. The doctor got out his jew's

harp, Jamie Prewitt his guitar, and Malcom Bentley his fiddle. The three of them played well into the night, and all of the settlers danced.

Jeremiah Mitchell was carried out so he could at least watch the dancing and hear the music, even if he couldn't participate. The doctor was pleased with how his foot was healing, and they were all thankful he shouldn't have to lose the foot.

Hannah found her energy for the dancing was better now that she'd been walking so much, and she didn't have to take any breaks.

Finally, as the men were finishing up for the night and everyone was turning in, Jed told Hannah to get a blanket, and they walked downriver from the camp-ground to enjoy some time together.

They sat and talked for a while, not really discussing anything of great importance, but they both talked of their hopes for the future. Jed talked of the church he wanted and the family atmosphere he wanted from the congregation. "And I want to have a good, solid farm. It doesn't have to be huge, but I want to have enough milk to make cheese and butter. I'll grow my own feed for the cows during the summer, and we'll have a big, red barn."

Hannah smiled, imagining it. "And we'll have a house with a small kitchen garden, and I'll grow carrots, potatoes, barley, and green beans. I want a white house, and I want it to have actual bedrooms. And I want a bathtub so I can take baths whenever I want. When you dig the well, I want it to be close to the house so I don't have to travel far to get the water for cooking and cleaning."

"Maybe we can find some nice rolling hills to live in. And raise children." He looked at her. "Do you want a lot of children?"

"I'd like at least four or five. I never did like being an only child, but my mother just never got pregnant again after me."

"So, if we're going to make lots of babies, do you think we should practice making them?"

Hannah laughed softly. "That sounds like a good idea to me." She moved to him readily on the blanket, knowing now what to expect. When her mother had first told her about the marriage bed, it hadn't sounded pleasant to her at all. But when she and Jed made love, it was a special experience.

It didn't take them long to lose their clothes and to again move together as if they were one. When they'd finished, he rolled off her to her side. "Tomorrow's going to be a hard day."

She nodded. "At least we know we'll be staying along the Wolf River tomorrow, and there won't be any need to look for more water for camping."

"That's true." He got up and put his clothes on, and she followed suit, walking back to camp with him. She yawned as he put up their tent, and she quickly grabbed her journal.

"I need to write about today before I forget." Hannah quickly scribbled out her thoughts for the day, and she tucked the journal back into her trunk. Then she caught the kittens who were snuggled together in the back of the wagon, and took them into the tent with her and Jed. She wanted them to stay warm as well, and they could snuggle with one of the humans if they needed to.

———

Rain hit the small group the following day for the first time since they'd left Independence. It was cold and dreary, and when they stopped around two in the afternoon, they were all chilled to the bone. Hannah quickly built up a fire, and she changed out of her wet clothes. "Someone's going to get sick from this," she said worriedly to Mary.

"I agree. We're all going to have to be extra careful to get warm tonight." Mary hurried off to join her family.

"I guess we're all doing beans tonight," Hannah said to no one in particular.

The visibility had been low due to the rain, and Mary hadn't been able to shoot any critters at all. Hannah was a little disappointed but she knew she would make it work. It was her job to provide good meals for her husband, and she had promised her mother she would do the best job she possibly could. She wouldn't bring shame on her family.

When Jed joined her, he immediately set up their tent, and Hannah huddled inside it as she waited for the beans to boil. It hadn't been easy to even get the fire started, and now she was going to have to cook in the rain. Somehow, she'd never imagined there would be rain on the Trail.

The mountains, the rivers, the cold...she'd been ready for all those things, but not for the rain. She said a quick prayer to thank God for giving them rain after they crossed the river and not before. She sincerely hoped the Platte wouldn't be too high when they got there, but she knew that was down the road.

There would certainly be no slipping away late at night to make love under the stars tonight, but perhaps the sound of the rain would make it okay to make love right there in camp.

Once they'd eaten, she washed the dishes by quickly rinsing them in the rain water from the opening of the tent. There was no camaraderie that evening as everyone tried to keep out of the freezing rain.

She wrote in her journal before taking the kittens into the tent with her and Jed, both of them shaking with the cold. She wished they had just one more blanket to add to the small pile covering them, but she wasn't sure where she'd get one from out here on the trail.

She fell asleep with Jed's arms wrapped around her, and she finally felt warm for the first time all day.

———

The following day they travelled along the Wolf River again, and they made good time. It was still muddy, and one of the wagons got stuck early in the morning, but the men worked together and got it going within an hour, and they simply moved later into the afternoon when possible.

They camped around five that day, and were all pleased to have left the cold rain behind them. The musicians once again took their instruments out, and a card game was organized. Hannah and Jed played against Mary and Bob Hastings. They played a game called Euchre, which neither Mary or Hannah had played, but Jed had played in Illinois growing up and Bob had played in Wisconsin.

The game was fun, if a bit complicated to learn. Mary and Bob were expert teammates, though, and they won each game, hands down.

After the game, Mary stole a few minutes with Hannah. "I think I saw buffalo tracks today. I cannot wait until I'm able to actually shoot one. It would feed the whole camp!"

"It would. And we could make jerky out of everything that's left."

Mary wrinkled her nose. "I hate making jerky, but I'd help, because you're my friend."

Hannah laughed. "So, what is going on between you and Mr. Hastings? Do you have feelings for him?"

"No. Absolutely not. Just because you're happily married doesn't mean I ever will be. No, you will not try to marry me off. I'm better alone." Mary shook her head emphatically.

"Are you sure?" Hannah asked. She was more teasing her friend than anything else.

"I'm sure. Trust me. I am not meant to marry."

When Hannah returned to camp, Jed had already prepared for bed. She joined him in their tent, and they listened to the campground, which was mostly quiet around them. "I had fun playing cards with them," Jed said softly, burying his face in her fiery hair. More than anything else about her, her hair fascinated him. It went down to almost her knees, and he wanted to wind it around his wrists.

"I'm glad. I like anything I do with Mary. She's a fun person. She is convinced she saw buffalo tracks today, and she wants to shoot her first buffalo. She said it'll feed the entire wagon train, and I told her I'd make jerky from what was left with her."

"That sounds good to me," Jed said. "I happen to be a big fan of jerky. You'll find a lot of it in the back of the wagon, but I'm trying not to use it. We need to be able to still eat when we get to Oregon."

"I'm doing my best to be very frugal with our food."

"How's Mrs. Bolling and the girls doing?"

"Better than I expected at first. Mrs. Bolling is a lot stronger than she looks. The girls are learning to play on the trail and not spend all of their time dreading the walking. It does help that they nap all afternoon every day." She hid a loud yawn behind her hand. "I can't believe I'm so tired."

"Tomorrow's Sunday," he said softly. "We'll have

church services right after lunchtime. That way the women can get the laundry washed in the morning, and hopefully it will be dry before nightfall. That's the plan anyway."

"What's your sermon on tomorrow?" she asked.

"Moses in the wilderness. I'm going to compare the meat we've been able to kill to manna from heaven."

"That sounds like something we all need. It should really be enjoyable." Hannah frowned. "I'm not looking forward to doing the laundry in a river."

"Well, of course not. I wouldn't be either, but the trail has hardships for all of us."

"I do feel like the men's work is done as soon as the wagons are stopped for the evening. The women keep working until after supper."

"I think the trail is much harder on you women than it is on men. I don't deny it. I'm just glad I have you with me. Hannah, I don't think you understand what you're coming to mean to me."

Hannah sighed happily. "I hope I mean as much to you as you're coming to mean to me." She'd been facing away from him, but she turned over and kissed him, his arms coming around her. "Let's just try to be quiet this time."

Jed nodded, deepening their kiss. If she wanted to stay there to make love, then he was happy to do it.

———

SUNDAY ENDED up being a good day to rest. The oxen needed a rest as much as the humans did. Hannah woke to the sound of the gunshot, and she immediately got a fire started and made coffee. Then she went down to the river to start the huge chore of doing laundry in a river.

Mary joined her soon after she started, and the two of

them together scrubbed clothes. Mary sang as she worked, and Hannah sat quietly listening to her friend. "I had no idea you could sing so well," she said when her friend became quiet.

Mary shrugged. "I don't like to really sing in front of people, but I do love singing. It's a mostly private thing. I'm really comfortable around you, so I can sing when it's just the two of us."

On both sides of them, there were women up and down the river working on their laundry.

When Mrs. Bolling finished her laundry, she hung it between two wagons to dry, but then she did something that surprised Hannah. "What are you doing?"

Mrs. Bolling simply smiled. "I want to thank you for your generosity. Give me a few minutes and then come see me."

Mrs. Bolling had been parking her wagon beside her and Jed's tent every night, because they had become friends. As soon as Hannah finished hanging the clothes, she walked to the other woman's wagon. Her hand immediately went over her mouth. "What have you done?"

"I brought my bathtub with me, and I filled it after heating some of the water. I want you and Miss Mitchell to have the first two baths because you both have done so much to help me."

Mrs. Bolling had put the tub between two wagons, and she'd hung sheets to hide the bathtub. "I'll charge everyone but you two."

Hannah didn't need to be told twice. "Bless you, Mrs. Bolling!"

"Please call me Margaret."

"Then you must call me Hannah."

"I'd be happy to." Margaret left the small enclosed area

she'd made, and Hannah stripped and got into the tub. She threw her dress over one of the blankets Margaret had hung to make her curtain, and she sank as deep into the water as she could.

Of course, the tub wasn't as nice as the one Hannah had used back home, but it was a far cry better than the freezing cold river which was her only other option.

She was careful not to take too long in the bath, because she knew Mary would want a turn while the water was still warm, and she needed to cook something for lunch for her husband.

After she'd dried off and gotten dressed, she walked back to her husband feeling like a new woman. "Margaret drew me a bath!" She was practically dancing with joy at the feeling of having all the dirt off her skin.

Jed smiled. "I helped her with the water."

"Oh, thank you! I've said it before and I'll say it again. You are the very best of husbands." She threw herself into his arms and held tight.

Jed laughed. "You're just happy because you're clean." He knew it had bothered her, but there had been nothing he could do about it until that morning.

"That's a lot of it."

"I have another surprise…"

"You cannot keep giving me presents!" Hannah protested.

"Oh, this is a present as much for me as it is for you." He pointed to a deer he had hanging upside down from a tree down by the river. "I thought it might be nice to have a good supper."

"May I share some with Margaret?" she asked, immediately thinking of her friend.

"You know, you are the very best of wives for a preacher. You always think of others first."

Hannah shook her head. "Not at all. I thought about how it would taste in a nice thick stew before I thought about my friend." She pursed her lips. "I'm going to invite Margaret and the girls to eat with us tonight if I may. She drives all day, cooks at night and still minds her children. She's doing men's and women's work every day."

"Yes, I think you should invite her for supper. It would be good for her and the girls to eat someone else's cooking for once. Dig deep in the food box, and I have a few potatoes and a few carrots. I didn't buy a lot, but they'll help to make a perfect meal for company."

She stood on tiptoe and kissed his cheek. "Thank you, Jed."

She got out the leftovers from the previous night, and for once was able to warm up their noon meal. Both of them ate quietly, and then he found a good place for his sermon. He sat on a rock, and the others crowded around, ready to receive a message about their God.

As Hannah watched him preach, her eyes were filled with love and praise for the man she was married to. His words filled her with hope, and she could see from the faces of the other emigrants that they were filled with hope as well.

After the sermon, several of the men shook his hand and thanked him for preaching. "I'll share the next meat I get with you, pastor."

"This morning, I was able to get a deer, so I'm set for tonight. But we're happy to take any meat you don't need." He smiled, obviously thankful that his words had an impact on so many different people there in the camp.

Many of the men went hunting that afternoon, and Jed

joined them, hoping to get a couple more deer or anything else that happened along. The more he could help Mrs. Bolling with food, the less Hannah would be worried about the other woman and her family.

Shortly after the men had left for their hunt, Margaret hurried over to Hannah. "I can't find Sally. She was sleeping in the wagon beside Amanda, but now she's missing. I need your help!"

Hannah nodded, and she called out to the other women and children who were left in camp. Mary had apparently gone on the hunt with the men, but all of the other women were still there, and they all started searching right away.

Margaret was beside herself with worry, crying hysterically. "What if she's out where the men are hunting? She could be accidentally shot."

"We're all looking everywhere, Margaret. I promise you she'll be found." Hannah hurried off, looking at all the wagons in the circle. When she'd reached back at the beginning wagon, which was Margaret's, she looked inside just to be sure the child hadn't returned when no one was looking.

Sure enough, little Sally was sleeping beside her sister. She called as loud as she could, "I found her!"

The other women came running, and she pointed into the wagon at the two little girls sleeping side by side.

Margaret was the first to arrive by her side, and she was still crying. "I think she's been there the whole time," Hannah said calmly, smiling at her friend. She couldn't imagine what terror would be felt by a mother with a lost child.

Margaret threw her arms around Hannah. "Oh, thank heavens. I thought I'd lost her for good."

"We're not going to let that happen," Hannah said. "That's why we're all traveling together."

The other women reassured her, and soon after, the camp had returned to its usual quiet when the men were away. "I'm fixing a venison stew tonight, and I'm making enough for your family and mine."

Margaret, who had finally calmed, burst out crying again. "I haven't done anything to help you, and you and the pastor have been so generous with me and my girls. I feel like I need to do something in return."

"You heated water for me to take a bath today!" Hannah said. "It was a comfort I didn't think I'd have until we got to Oregon. How can you say you've done nothing for me?"

Margaret smiled. "I did that to thank you, and here you are doing more to thank *me*. I am so glad this was the wagon train I chose. It's like having a sister right here with me. You and Mary have both made my life so much easier since the trip started."

Hannah nodded. "And when you think about it, the trip is still a great deal harder for you than for anyone else. You're doing men's and women's work every day."

"But that's because my husband died. I *should* have to do both."

"No, you shouldn't. The Bible says we need to help the widows and orphans, and you and your children are both. We will help you. I'd quote the actual scripture, but I don't remember where it is. I wish Jed was here!"

Margaret smiled. "Don't worry about that. Why don't we cook supper together? I'll help you chop the vegetables and do whatever else you plan to do while the girls sleep. Maybe this evening I can simply spend some time with my babies and not worry about anything else."

"That sounds good to me. Are any of the men bringing you meat in exchange for meals yet? Jed said he'd tell everyone you were willing."

"Not yet. But you and Mary have made sure I had meat if anyone did. I'm sure they will further on down the road." Margaret looked a bit skeptical about whether she and her girls would actually make it, but Hannah was determined if they could survive that they *would*.

When the men came back to camp, Hannah's stew was simmering over the fire. Jed walked over and smiled. "That smells so good!"

"Margaret had some spices we added to the pot," she said.

"Well, thank you, Margaret! You're supposed to be resting tonight so that Hannah could cook for you."

"Well, I'm going to rest and spend time with my girls after I finish helping Hannah with the supper dishes."

Hannah turned from the fire. "I let you help me cook, but you are not going to help me with the dishes. You spend all the time you can with your girls. You'll have enough to do tomorrow."

Margaret looked conflicted for a moment, and then she smiled. "I'm thankful, Hannah."

"Don't worry about it. We love the idea of helping you." Jed smiled at his wife, realizing that she really was the perfect preacher's wife. The way he had found her was ridiculous. Her step-father had been wanting to all but sell her, which he was sure Hannah didn't realize. Well, it wasn't really selling her, because Jed had been paid to take her away.

The stew turned out beautifully, and Margaret made biscuits to go with the meal. When the pastor prayed over the meal, he made sure to mention how thankful he was to be able to share the meal with a special family.

Little Sally looked around her. "What special family?"

Hannah laughed and poked the little girl's belly. "Your

special family. We're feeling happy that you're allowing us to eat with you!"

After supper, Hannah shooed Margaret and her girls away. "I will come get the girls in the morning before we start out again."

"You are such a blessing to me, Hannah. I do hope you know that."

As Hannah watched the young widow lead her children away, she said to Jed, "I was certain I would be a horrible pastor's wife. I thought I would make everyone think less of you in the beginning. I think I'm doing all right."

"You are definitely doing all right. You're the perfect wife for me in every way. At first, I wondered about your upbringing, because you had obviously had a much more privileged upbringing than most. But I was wrong, because you are better with people and more loving than any pastor's wife, I've ever seen."

Hannah felt tears pop into her eyes at his words. She was doing something right to get that kind of praise from her husband. He wasn't one to praise lightly.

When she wrote in her journal, she mentioned how thankful she was for the man she'd married. He truly was the man she needed in her life.

NINE

I DON'T KNOW how I went through my entire life without Jed at my side. All of my feelings of aloneness that I've had since my father died have disappeared, and I certainly thank God for him every single day of my life.

We are now camped at the Nemaha River, and we have plenty of water and wood here. The stream is as clear and as cold as ice. This area is one of the most beautiful I have ever seen. I think if I had my choice, I would live here for the rest of my days, as the beauty is mesmerizing. As difficult as this journey is, I feel like it is making memories that I will treasure for the rest of my life.

I look at the world differently now, wanting to be the best wife I can possibly be. I was thinking about sewing myself a split skirt for this journey, but I've decided against it. I want to do all I can to uphold the goodness that is my husband and his reputation.

The days turned into one another as they continued

their trek toward Oregon, and every day Hannah fell just a little more in love with the man she married.

The four single men had taken to providing Margaret with meat every night in turn, and they would all eat with her. It seemed to Hannah that Jamie was taken with the sweet woman, but she didn't say that to Margaret. She knew her friend was still mourning her husband, and it wouldn't be fair to put notions like that in her head.

Hannah would watch the men bring her the meat they wanted her to cook, and Margaret's face would always light up, and she would thank them for their kindness to her family. It was obvious the men were all happy to do something for her, because she truly was a wonderful cook.

Every morning when Hannah woke, she would make the coffee, and then get the girls ready for their day of walking. She helped Margaret out in every way she could, but she refused to neglect her husband to do so.

At the end of the day on Saturday, they gathered around to talk about their plans for the next week. Captain Bedwell told them all that they hoped to be at the Platte in another two weeks. "I hope you will all be ready early in the morning and be ready for long, hard days. I do not want us to get behind schedule and miss out on finding our land this year. At this point, we're following our schedule perfectly. Let's keep doing so."

Hannah looked forward to seeing the milestone Platte River. She'd heard so much about it as they'd talked about it a lot on the trail. She turned to Jed who stood beside her and smiled. "We've made it two weeks, and we haven't even died of dysentery."

"Why would we die of dysentery?" he asked, confused.

"I have no idea, but I've heard people are nervous about it." Hannah hurried off to fix their supper, thankful the next day was Sunday and their day off. She wished they had two storage barrels for water and not just one. Somehow, she felt the need to hoard water.

As soon as she finished making venison steaks with biscuits, she sat back and waited for Jed to return from helping the other men round up the cattle and make sure they were all close by. It was his turn to stand guard for the first half of the night, and she was going to miss having him sleep beside her.

The kittens were doing well, growing more each day. They looked like totally different creatures than the ones he'd handed her back in Independence.

She gave the kittens some of the buttermilk that was left after she'd made butter that day. Of course, making butter on the trail was a million times easier than making it back in Independence. She simply hung her pail of cream under the wagon, and it was butter by noontime. The wagon ride was so bumpy, she felt sorry for people who didn't *get* to walk.

When she'd finished with the kittens, got some mending out. Jed had ripped a button off his shirt, and it needed to be fixed, because he only had three shirts with him.

When he joined her, they ate supper together. "Are you worried about standing guard this evening?" she asked. "There haven't been any Indian sightings have there?"

"We've seen a few here and there, but no one has come close enough to the camp to bother us. If you want to give me one of the dresses you're willing to trade, I'll keep it with me tonight in case we're approached by some."

Hannah nodded. "I'll make sure you get a dress after supper. Who are you standing guard with?"

"Mr. Mitchell. He'll always be my partner when I stand guard, which will be about every two weeks. They offered to not make me help with guard duty, because I'm the preacher, but I am young, and I can handle both. It's better to let the older men who need to preserve their strength sleep."

"That makes sense to me. I hate that you have to pull double duty, but I know you're strong enough to do it." She looked down at her plate. "I'll miss having you hold me as I fall asleep tonight."

"I'll miss you too. It's only for four hours, though, and then I'll be able to join you."

"What are you going to preach about tomorrow?" she asked.

"I thought about preaching about the different ways God provides for us. He makes sure we get to rivers when necessary, and he has provided meat for us almost every night. Our group is strong, and there's only been one serious injury so far. We've been blessed."

"We have," she said with a smile. "I feel like we've been blessed by God with both the way he's delivered us through, but also how wonderful our new friends are. I hate the idea that we won't see them anymore after we get to Oregon. Do you think we can talk them all into settling in the same area with us once we arrive?"

He laughed. "I really don't think that's possible."

A short while after Jed went to start his guard duty, Hannah saw a teenage girl pass by with a peppermint stick in her cleavage. She went to Amanda's wagon. Hannah had met her, and knew her name was Edna Blue, but they were always ahead of them in the order of the wagons, so she hadn't gotten to know her. It did seem odd that she was walking about with that peppermint stick coming up out of the front of her dress, but the girl had been dressed the same every time she'd seen her. Perhaps she thought to start a fashion that way.

She shook her head and got Edna out of her thoughts, going to the river for water to wash their dishes. The music was starting for dancing that evening, but without Jed to dance with her, she chose instead to work on the laundry tonight, so it would have all day tomorrow to dry.

She was the only one at the river while she was scrubbing the clothes, but she thought she could see another couple sneaking by. Squinting her eyes into the darkness, it looked like Mary, but who would Mary be sneaking around the camp with? Mary hadn't mentioned to Hannah a man she was interested in, and she still said she planned to homestead on her own. It was odd.

Hannah finished the clothes and hung them to dry, thankful that hated part of her week was over. Washing in the dark wasn't something she ever wanted to do.

She walked back to camp and lay down in the tent that Jed had erected for her before he left, and she wrote in her journal in the tent, and when she was finished, she closed her eyes and let the music wash over her.

The kittens wrestled in the tent beside her, as they always did late at night. They had taken to killing birds during the day and bringing the dead critters to drop them at her feet. More than once she'd stepped on one, and she always gave an unladylike squeal when she did.

When Jed returned to the tent, he found his wife sleeping peacefully and decided not to wake her, though he would have liked to. He lay down beside her, wrapping one arm around her and snuggling her close to him.

Sunday morning was a lazy morning for Hannah, because she had done most of her work for the day the previous evening. She woke before the gunshot, and she turned over to find Jed behind her.

She kissed his neck and woke him without meaning to. His brown eyes stared into her green. "You seem awake," he said.

She nodded. "I fell asleep early because I missed you. I can get up."

He shook his head, and flipped her onto her back, kissing her passionately. "Why would I want you to do that?"

She wrapped her arms around his neck and held onto him as he gently explored her body. She had no idea what time it was, but she certainly hoped they could do what they needed to do before the other emigrants woke.

They had just finished when the gunshot sounded, and the camp started to stir around them. She giggled, and he kissed the sound away, but when he lifted his head he was grinning as big as she was. "If they could have just waited another minute or two..."

"I'm glad they weren't a minute or two earlier," she whispered back. She bounced off the ground and pulled her clothes on. "I'll start the coffee." She decided that starting her day with a romp in the covers with Jed was the perfect way to stay happy.

"I may need to take a nap after services while all the other men are hunting."

"I might nap with you," she said wiggling her eyebrows at him. "I did the laundry last night, so there's no need for me to work all day today." There were still meals to prepare, of course, but the bulk of her work for the day was finished.

"Good!" he said. "I'm never going to refuse a nap with my beautiful wife."

She frowned and walked out to start the fire. She didn't

like it when he called her beautiful, because it always made her feel like he was talking about another woman. That wasn't what she wanted from her husband.

He came out just as she was putting the coffee on the fire, and he sat down beside her on the ground. "Did I say something to bother you?"

She shrugged. "I just don't like it when you call me beautiful. I know I'm not beautiful, and I always feel you must be thinking about another woman when you say those things."

"You really don't think you're beautiful?" he asked, stunned. From the day he'd met her, he'd admired her hair, but the more he'd gotten to know her, the more kindness radiated from every pore of her body.

"I really know I'm not beautiful. So please don't say that again."

He frowned. "I say what I see."

"Please." She turned away and stirred the campfire, putting a pan on the fire to heat for flapjacks. She was finished talking about her appearance. He was a handsome man, and she always felt as if she'd married a man meant for another.

He sat and watched her for a while, admiring her appearance. He so wished she could see herself through his eyes, and realize what a treasure he'd found when he walked into her home that first night.

Instead of sitting there, he got up and walked, taking the musket with him. He never knew when he might see an animal that would be good in Hannah's stew pot, so he always went prepared. He enjoyed the variation the different types of meat brought as much as she enjoyed cooking with new things.

He had walked a good mile away from camp when he

saw a herd of buffalo out of the corner of one eye. He wasn't certain if he should run back to camp or run toward them and try to shoot. Deciding he had a better chance of bringing one of the great beasts down if he didn't go back to camp, he ran toward them, his musket against one shoulder.

When he was close enough, he took careful aim and one of the buffalo fell. It wasn't quite weak enough, and tried to run again, so one more shot had it laying dead on the ground, while the rest of the herd kept running.

He turned to run back to camp, but his gunfire had brought several of the men, who went with him to fetch his kill. "This will feed the entire camp tonight," one of the men said.

Another raised his musket to shoot another, but Jed said softly, "Why kill another when we won't be able to eat all of the meat from this one? Another would just go to waste."

"He's right," Mr. Mitchell said. "We don't need to be wasteful with the buffalo. One is enough for the whole camp for a couple of days. The women will work on drying it, and we'll all feast tonight."

Jed was glad to have another man back him up. He wanted to leave the land as pristine as they'd found it, not littered with rotten buffalo carcasses.

The men quickly went to work on the dead buffalo as soon as the herd was past. They skinned it, cut it up, and carried the meat back to camp. It took hours to get that much meat into small chunks, but they knew the meals they would all get from it would be worth it.

Jed carried a choice roast back to camp and presented it to Hannah. For a moment, she looked repulsed, and he remembered her background. Then she took the meat from him and put it in the Dutch Oven she had, and put the pot right into the fire. "Buffalo?" she asked after the meat was settled.

He grinned. His pampered wife was learning to act first and ask questions later. "Yes. I shot it."

She smiled up at him. "Mary is going to be disappointed. She wanted to be the first in the train to kill a buffalo."

"Well, she can help dry the leftover meat then. There's more than enough to feed the entire wagon train with a lot left over."

"Oh, wonderful! I will help with the drying since I've finished my laundry already." Of course, that would have to wait until after the noon meal, and the church service he would have for them all.

He nodded, pleased that she seemed to be in better spirits than she had been when he'd walked out of camp a short while before. He reached for another cup of coffee and took a drink. He'd noticed a lot of the other emigrants had started to drink water, and while it sounded wonderfully refreshing to him, he didn't want to risk his health that way.

Sure enough, by noon, one of the women he barely knew was sick that day. "We'll pray for your wife," he promised Mr. Henderson before the church services. By the time the services were over, they were digging a deep grave for the woman. Cholera took people quickly, and cholera was exactly what Mrs. Henderson had been diagnosed with.

Dr. Bentley urged them all to begin drinking coffee, even the small children. "We don't know why it is, but people who drink coffee on the trail don't get sick and people who don't often die. Please everyone, drink coffee and not water."

It was the first death in their wagon train, and all of them were hit hard by the news. It shouldn't have been unexpected, but somehow it was, and they were all shocked by her death. It had taken almost two weeks for them to lose one of their own, but the others who had died from previous wagon trains weren't living breathing people to them, and Mrs. Henderson had been.

Her husband and three children walked around camp looking lost without her. The children were all quite young, the oldest being seven years old. When Hannah saw them just after the funeral, she stopped and took Mr. Henderson's hand consolingly. "If you would like, I'll make sure your children walk with me every day from now on. There's no need for you to fret about them while you're driving your wagon."

The man nodded, but seemed unable to say anything else. He was obviously devastated by the quick, unexpected death of his wife.

The children were all looking lost and confused. Hannah walked with him so she could introduce herself. "I'm Mrs. Scott. I'll be walking with you starting tomorrow."

"Your husband is the preacher," the tallest one, a boy, said to her.

"He is. What's your name?"

"I'm David, these are Hattie and Alice. They're little, and I don't think they understand." David swiped at a tear on his cheek, angry that he was showing the emotion. "I'm seven. Hattie is four and Alice is two. They need a mama."

"They do," Hannah said softly. "I'm sure their papa will do what's right for them, though."

"What's right for them?" David asked, his face earnest.

"Your papa will know, even if you and I don't." Hannah

looked at Mr. Henderson. "I have enough meat to make a huge meal tonight. Please come and eat with us, if you can."

"I don't want to be around people," was all Mr. Henderson said. She could see by the look on his face that he was devastated to have lost his wife.

"Then I'll bring some food to you, and you can eat it or not. I do think your children should eat."

He nodded, and she turned and walked away, and the further she got away, the more she wanted to run and hide. And she did. She ran from camp and continued downstream for as far as she could run, and then she fell to her knees. Mrs. Henderson had not been someone she really knew, but the entire wagon train was her community. And her heart went out to those precious children who had lost the most important person in their world. She couldn't stop thinking back to the death of her own father, and the tears wouldn't stop. Even after she'd pulled her special hanky from her sleeve and used it for the tears, she couldn't seem to stop her ridiculous reaction.

Jed found her, far from camp, kneeling in the dirt crying, and he simply put his arm around her and held her as she wept. He didn't necessarily understand her upset, but he didn't need to. She was bereft at the death of a stranger, and she couldn't stop crying, and it was his job to be strong for her. For the entire wagon train. She was his wife, and he would see to it that nothing terrible happened to her again.

They went back to camp when she'd calmed herself, and she put on potatoes and carrots to go with the roast. She was determined to make the best meal she possibly could for those precious children and their father.

Jed sat beside her, watching her work. "Do you want to talk about it?"

At his questions, her tears started again. She couldn't

speak because she was so upset, she was beyond words. Seeing those children, shortly after their mother had died so quickly, had been too much.

She wanted desperately to explain to him why she was so unhappy, but she truly didn't have the words. Later she'd be able to speak, or so she hoped.

As the day wore on, she found herself completely incapable of speaking to anyone. Mary came by, and when she asked her why she was sad, Hannah started crying once again, shaking her head when the words wouldn't come.

Once supper was cooked, she took a portion for her and her husband, and she handed him the pot and nodded in the direction of the Hendersons' wagon, hoping he'd know he was supposed to carry it over to the other family.

"I'll take this to the Hendersons," he said. "They'll have food to eat on this most difficult of nights."

She nodded, and she sat waiting for him to return before she ate. As soon as he was back, he took her hand and prayed over their meal for them, asking God to help Hannah with whatever was making her so terribly sad.

As she ate the meal she'd fixed, she thought about the laundry Mrs. Henderson had done that morning. She'd seen her working on it when the stomach ailment hit her. After supper, she would go over and take down the laundry and fold it for the bereft family.

When she stood to go to them, Jed took her arm, shaking his head. "No. You can't go there and help them. You can't even help yourself right now."

She nodded, but she wasn't pleased with his answer. She had never been an obedient woman, but it didn't take her long to know he was completely right at that moment. She couldn't go there and cry as if she'd been best friends with Mrs. Henderson, because she hadn't. Not at all. She loved her in a way that all Christians should love others, but her reaction was much worse than it should have been.

She washed the supper dishes, and sat down in front of the fire with her arms wrapped around her legs. Hannah realized she didn't want to go on. She wanted to sit there in that camp and watch over Mrs. Henderson's grave. She didn't know the woman's first name, but she still felt the need to protect her and be with her.

Her family would move on the following day and not even have a gravestone to visit to remember her. There was no gravestone. There was no cross. She was buried in a patch of dirt right on the Oregon Trail. Tomorrow when the wagons rolled over that spot, the dirt would be pressed down, and it wouldn't be obvious that anyone had even died.

Hannah knew it was a necessity to do things that way, because the animals couldn't really smell her that way, and the Indians wouldn't work that hard to find her scalp, but Mrs. Henderson deserved better than that. Hannah wanted to rant and rave and scream her sorrow for the ignominious burial the other woman had received but not deserved. Her children were well-dressed, and they obviously loved their mother. How could a woman who was loved so well by their children ever deserve for that to happen?

Jed put up the tent early, and she didn't even question him wanting her to go in there. What she was feeling would make no sense to others, but it made perfect sense to her. She had lost her father just as unexpectedly, and now she had neither parent to love or care for. She was as lost to the people she'd always known as Mrs. Henderson was.

Why had she married and left Independence, when she knew that's where she needed to be? She loved Jed, and she hadn't regretted leaving with him before that moment. And now? All she could think about was if her mother died, she needed to have a decent burial with a headstone. If she wasn't there, who would see to it?

Long into the night, her tears were still falling, and she fell asleep while still crying hysterically.

Jed lay beside her, but he could sense she didn't want his words, and even more she didn't want his touch. Once she was asleep, he pulled the covers over them both and he draped his arm around her. He wished he could find the words she obviously needed to feel better, but he didn't have them inside him.

He was awake long after her breathing became even, because he wanted to help her, and all he could think to do was pray, and he prayed with all his might that the Hendersons would find peace, but more than that, he prayed that his wife would find a way to get past her sorrow over the death of a stranger.

If anyone had ever needed a miracle, he needed one at that moment.

TEN

Jed's Journal

I'M NOT certain what to do at this moment. We had our first cholera death from our wagon train yesterday, and we lost a young mother with three small children. She was someone neither of us knew well by the name of Nellie Henderson. She was sick at noon, and we buried her before three in the afternoon. Her death was quick and saddening.

Also, yesterday, I was the first to get a buffalo from our wagon train. My wife made a beautiful roast with carrots and potatoes, and she had me take it to the family. Before that happened, though, she introduced herself to the husband and all three children. The children will now walk with my wife every day, while I drive our wagon. Her life is going to be more difficult because she has so much compassion for these people.

When she had spoken to them, she turned and ran from

the camp, crying hysterically. She must have run a mile, and this from a woman who tells me her feet ache on a daily basis. She had a day when she didn't have to walk the trail, and instead she ran a mile back before sinking to her knees and sobbing hysterically. She has been unable to speak since that moment.

I do not know how to help her, and I have prayed and prayed. I have been up all night trying to think of what I could do to take the burden of her sorrow from her. I cannot come up with a solution. I pray God tells me what to do for her, so I can continue to have my bride on my side.

I am afraid she will find her voice again and beg for me to take her back to Independence. I would not want to, but I would do it and stay there with her if need be. She is a great deal more important to me than free land in Oregon.

I pray it won't come to that.

Hannah was still in a daze most of the next day. Thankfully Mary took the children who usually walked with her under her wing and watched out for them. She kept trying to talk to Hannah, but Hannah didn't find herself capable of doing anything more than going through the motions of their journey. She made breakfast, walked, ate lunch, but forgot to take Jed his lunch, and she fixed supper.

She did everything she knew she had to do, but she did nothing more. She didn't speak to anyone, and she didn't know if she would be able to anytime soon.

When Jed came to her at supper, he spoke to her using a soft voice, and tried to get her to talk to him. She looked at him, and she opened her mouth, but no words came out, and the tears came back into her eyes.

She made extra supper again, thanks to the buffalo he'd killed the day before, and he took the extra over to the Hendersons. When he returned, he told her they needed to go for a walk so they could talk, and she simply nodded, willing to agree to anything. There was nothing left inside her but sorrow, so it was easy to go along with him.

As they walked, he tried again to speak to her. "Hannah, I'm getting really worried about you. Are you feeling ill?"

She shook her head.

"Are you angry with me for something?"

Hannah again shook her head, more emphatically this time.

"I need to know what's happening. Why have you stopped speaking?"

She opened her mouth and tried to speak, but the words seemed to catch in her throat, and she was unable to force them out, even after putting a hand to her neck and trying to force them out of her mouth.

He took a deep breath. "Are you willing to continue toward Oregon?"

She stopped walking and looked at him for a moment. She didn't know if she was willing to keep going. Did he want to take her back to Independence? Was she too defective to continue along the trail?

"Do you want to go back to Independence and live with your parents?" he asked, hoping she would be able to respond to something.

She shook her head.

"Do you want to go back to Independence to live with me?"

She wasn't sure how to answer that question either. She put her hands in the air, face up, to express that she just didn't know. On one hand, she wanted to run away from the trials and death that came with life on the Trail. On the other, she wanted to continue on with him, to prove to herself she could do it.

When they got back to camp, Jed went to fetch the doctor, determined that a cure for her would be found, whatever it was that was wrong. When the doctor approached Hannah, she waved him away, but Jed refused to let him leave.

"She hasn't spoken since yesterday afternoon. I've seen her open her mouth and try to speak, but nothing comes out. You have to find out what's wrong with her."

The doctor frowned, but he put a hand on either side of her throat. "Open your mouth."

Hannah did everything she was told to do.

"I can't find anything wrong with her." Dr. Bentley frowned at Hannah. "Hannah, why won't you speak?"

Hannah immediately started crying again. She couldn't explain her deep sorrow at the other woman's death. She didn't know *how* to explain, but she knew that Jed wasn't going to rest until he knew.

Instead of trying to speak again, Hannah let the men talk, and she walked to her journal and wrote.

I'm not sure why I'm so upset at the passing of Mrs. Henderson, because I barely knew her. I was fine until I looked into the eyes of those precious children, and I thought about them never having a mother. I thought about the wagon wheels going over her grave, and I even understand the reasoning behind it, but I can't help that it shattered my heart when it happened.

I think about her grave, devoid of headstone, and I think about those children who all loved their mother dearly who will now spend the rest of their lives wondering if she would have been proud of the things they do. They'll wonder if she would have been happy with their choice of a woman or man to marry. They'll wonder if she'd have been proud of their professions and their avocations.

Those children lost part of themselves yesterday, and it was a big important part of themselves, and I mourn for them. I mourn for myself because I lost my father in an instant, just as they lost their mother.

I mourn for myself because I will never again see my mother to know if she's proud of me. I will never again visit the headstone of the father who was one of the most important people in my life, and whom I miss dearly. I miss him every day. I miss him every hour.

Since I've met you, I've often forgotten to miss him though. He hasn't been on my mind as much as he once was, and I feel like I'm forsaking that memory. I looked into those children's eyes, and I knew they were just like me. I wanted to take their pain from them, but the very thought of their pain was too much for me to bear.

Yesterday changed four lives in a way that can never be mended. I want to mend those lives, but she's twenty miles behind us on the trail, and her body will remain there forever, even as her heart travels with her children.

I try to talk, but the sorrow is so overwhelming that the words will not move past my throat. I do not mourn for Mrs. Henderson. I mourn for her children and the mother they have lost.

Yesterday those three darling children woke up to a mother who made their breakfast, washed their clothes, and fixed their lunch. She was dead before she had a chance to fix their supper. I mourn for them. I mourn for my father, but mostly I mourn for myself.

Please give me time to do what needs to be done, and to get myself back to where I need to be. Only time can heal the *deep sorrow that has washed over me. I will do what I need to do in the meantime, but I may not be able to speak.*

When she'd finished writing the passage in her journal, she carried it to her husband, and showed him where to start reading. The doctor had already left, which pleased her, because she didn't want him checking on her. She wasn't *sick*. Her heart was shattered into a million pieces. And that was entirely different.

Jed carefully read everything that Hannah had written, and when he was finished, he felt he finally understood. "You feel guilty for leaving your father's grave, and it's bringing back his death all over again."

Hannah nodded emphatically, and took the journal back, thinking there was one more thing she could write that would help him understand.

I wonder if us being on the trail helped contribute to her death. If there hadn't been a pastor on the trail, would she have still gone? And would she have died? Is the trail just a long march to our deaths? Will we come out alive and if we don't, what will become of the children I know we are meant to have?

Jed read the last of what she wrote, and nodded. "Let's go in the tent and talk." It wouldn't keep people from being able to hear them, but it would keep them from seeing her. "I don't think we have any responsibility in the death of Mrs. Henderson. She made her choices. Even if the choice was out of her hands, and her husband ordered her to follow him, she made the decision to do as she was told, and the responsibility ultimately lies with her."

Hannah nodded. What he'd said made sense to her.

"We are not on a death march. I do know people who have made it safely to Oregon, and those people live there happily now that they've arrived. Even Captain Bedwell has been there and says we need to go. I think we will not be giving God everything we should give him if we don't make the trip. I can minister there in a way I truly can't in the east. I can do His work in a way that I've always dreamed of doing. Do you believe that's a good reason to endure hardship? For our God?"

Hannah nodded. She did believe so. But did that mean they wouldn't be culpable if they were meant to have children and they didn't?

"Then what we need to do is put our future and our children's future into God's hands. We cannot give him our worries and our fears and constantly take them back from him when we want to. We need to place them entirely in his hands forever." Jed took Hannah's hands in his own. "I know this has been a hard two weeks, and there will be many more hardships on the trail. I won't lie to you about that. This trail is one of blood and many tears, but I believe this is the way God wants us to go. So, I will go there. Do you want to go with me?"

Her eyes were filled with tears as she nodded. "I want to go."

At the sound of her voice—even though it was filled with tears—he felt something break inside him. Pulling her close he held her and stroked her hair. "I have been so worried about you, Hannah." He was so relieved to hear her speak, even though he knew she was still suffering.

She sniffled, feeling the torrent of tears coming again, but she knew she would be able to function again. She could speak, and she would continue doing so. Maybe she couldn't do it for herself, or even for the Henderson children. But she could do it for her Jed and for her God.

Settling down into their makeshift bed, Jed pulled her against him and held her, continually stroking her as she wept herself out. His touch had no sexual quality to it. He was a man who was doing everything he could to sooth the woman he loved beyond belief. And as soon as she was ready to hear it, he would tell her how very much he loved her, and he prayed she would say the words back to him.

Never in his life had he imagined he would fall in love with a woman as he had with Hannah. She completed him as no other woman really could. He wanted to kick himself for putting her through the sorrow she was experiencing, but he knew her place was there with him. And what's more, he knew she knew her place was there with him as well.

———

ON WEDNESDAY OF THAT WEEK, Mary and one of the men were able to get four antelope, which was more than enough to feed their entire wagon train. Hannah fixed meals for her and Jed and the Henderson family, who had started walking with her for the past two days.

When she'd finished the meal, she gave the Hendersons' portion to Jed, and he carried it to their wagon, which had begun parking on the other side of Margaret's wagon, because it was easier for Hannah to deal with the children and get meals to them.

When Jed returned to camp, he took his plate and Hannah's and told her to grab a blanket, because they were having a picnic dinner. She had no idea why he wanted to have a picnic when to her, every meal she'd ever eaten with him, save two that had happened at her mother's house, had been picnics.

She grabbed the blanket and followed him though, and he stopped at a spot under a tree, and she spread the blanket as he wanted. She sat down and took both plates so he could sit on the blanket as well.

She wasn't paying attention as he went to sit, and he sat down and handed her a bouquet of wildflowers. "Oh, Jed. They're lovely. Thank you!" He'd never given her flowers, but he'd never really had the opportunity to do so.

"Do you think those flowers are any less pretty because they aren't roses?" he asked.

"Of course not. That makes no sense."

"Well, what if I said there are women who are roses, and yes they're beautiful, but they're not always the flower that attracts you the most. What if I said a wildflower is a great deal prettier to me than a rose?"

She shrugged. "I don't see that being a problem." She had no idea what he was trying to say to her.

"To me, you're a wildflower, Hannah. You're not a rose like many of the women in the east think they are. You're a woman who has a unique beauty all your own. You are the most beautiful of women to me. Because you look different. Because your inner beauty shines in everything you do. The past few days have been very hard for you, but you never once failed to make a meal. You never once failed to cook for a family that just lost its mother. You're a beautiful woman, because what you do makes you beautiful."

She sat for a moment thinking about what he'd said. "So, when you tell me I'm beautiful, you really aren't lying?"

He shook his head. "I would never lie to you, Hannah. Your inner beauty is something like I've never seen before. I love the inside of you and the outside of you."

She slowly nodded, smiling. "I love you too, Jed. I love you so much! I'm sorry I wasn't really communicating with you when I got so upset, but I needed time to work through exactly what I was feeling. Now that I've taken that time, I know I'm where I need to be. On the trail to Oregon with you at my side."

Jed smiled. "I'm glad. I told myself that if you needed to go back to Independence to be able to smile again, then I would take you back to Independence. I would live there with you for the rest of my days if that's what you needed to be happy."

"It's not what I want. I needed to come to understand that no matter where you are, and no matter what you do, if you are doing your best to follow God's Word, then you are doing the right thing. We are doing the right thing. God will bless us for that."

"I agree with you." He took a bite of his supper, and smiled. "Wonderful supper as always. It's hard to believe it was less than three weeks ago that I first laid eyes on you, and you were convinced you would never be able to cook over a campfire. Look at you now!"

She laughed. "I had Mary and Margaret to help me. They are wonderful people, you know."

"I do know that. They've helped you in a way I never imagined when I first met you. Now you can shoot a musket, and you can skin a rabbit like it's nothing. And the kittens! They've grown so much, and you've managed to train them to follow along with you."

"I don't know that I trained them. They just know I'll feed them, so they keep following."

He smiled. "Well, either way they follow us. We're not going to have any mice problems when we get to Oregon, you know."

Hannah nodded emphatically. "I do know that. No mouse problems. No bird problems. I think if they worked as a team, they could take down a squirrel. Or even a buffalo!"

"I think the buffalo might be out of the question for them," he said with a smile.

"You're wrong. If I could keep going after how I felt on Sunday, then those two kittens can take down a buffalo."

"You know we're going to have dozens of children, and someday, they're going to read those journals we keep scribbling in, right?"

"Do you think they'll ever make a game about the Oregon Trail? Where everyone dies of dysentery?"

"They might," Jed said, looking at her strangely. "But it would make more sense if the game had them dying of cholera. Dysentery isn't nearly the killer on the trail that cholera is."

"I guess so. Still, in a hundred years or so, they may think that dysentery is the killer."

"Maybe so." He leaned forward and kissed her softly. "I just hope in a hundred or even two hundred years, people realize that the people on the Oregon Trail were real people, who went through hardships to get where they were going."

ABOUT THE AUTHOR

www.kirstenandmorganna.com

Made in the USA
Middletown, DE
08 April 2023

28498322R00087